HAUNTED HAPPINESS

Ravishing Marigold St. Aubrey knew what it was to love and to be loved. But two years had passed since her love had died in battle. And now her heart was under siege by his dashing and determined best friend, Sir Christopher Carlyon.

Mally knew she could never love Christopher as she had loved before—but how could she resist this suitor who was as handsome and ardent as he was wealthy and well-born?

Christopher himself knew it as well—and fought a losing struggle against his rising jealousy of a memory that would not let Mally free.

Love meant danger the second time around for a woman and a man who should have been the perfect pair—except for the haunting memory that threatened to divide them forever. . . .

MALLY

PAPERBACK EXCHANGE
BURTON SHOPPING CENTER
LA VALE, MARYLAND 21502
301-729-8100

SIGNET Regency Romances You'll Enjoy

- [ ] **THE SMUGGLER'S DAUGHTER** by Sandra Heath.
  (#E8816—$1.75)*
- [ ] **THE COUNTERFEIT MARRIAGE** by Joan Wolf.
  (#E9064—$1.75)*
- [ ] **A KIND OF HONOR** by Joan Wolf. (#E9296—$1.75)*
- [ ] **THE REBEL BRIDE** by Catherine Coulter. (#E8951—$1.75)*
- [ ] **THE AUTUMN COUNTESS** by Catherine Coulter.
  (#E8463—$1.75)*
- [ ] **LORD DEVERILL'S HEIR** by Catherine Coulter.
  (#E9200—$1.75)*
- [ ] **THE DUTIFUL DAUGHTER** by Vanessa Gray.
  (#E9017—$1.75)*
- [ ] **THE MASKED HEIRESS** by Vanessa Gray. (#E9331—$1.75)
- [ ] **THE WICKED GUARDIAN** by Vanessa Gray. (#E8390—$1.75)
- [ ] **THE INCOMPARABLE MISS BRADY** by Sheila Walsh.
  (#E9245—$1.75)*
- [ ] **MADALENA** by Sheila Walsh. (#E9332—$1.75)
- [ ] **THE GOLDEN SONG BIRD** by Sheila Walsh. (#E8155—$1.75)†
- [ ] **THE SERGEANT MAJOR'S DAUGHTER** by Sheila Walsh.
  (#E8220—$1.75)
- [ ] **BORROWED PLUMES** by Roseleen Milne. (#E8113—$1.75)†
- [ ] **THE MONTAGUE SCANDAL** by Judith Harkness.
  (#E8922—$1.75)*
- [ ] **THE ADMIRAL'S DAUGHTER** by Judith Harkness.
  (#E9161—$1.75)*

* Price slightly higher in Canada
† Not available in Canada

Buy them at your local bookstore or use this convenient coupon for ordering.

THE NEW AMERICAN LIBRARY, INC.,
P.O. Box 999, Bergenfield, New Jersey 07621

Please send me the SIGNET BOOKS I have checked above. I am enclosing
$_____ (please add 50¢ to this order to cover postage and handling).
Send check or money order—no cash or C.O.D.'s. Prices and numbers are
subject to change without notice.

Name _____

Address _____

City_____ State_____ Zip Code_____
Allow 4-6 weeks for delivery.
This offer is subject to withdrawal without notice.

MALLY
◎ *by* ◎
SANDRA HEATH

A SIGNET BOOK
NEW AMERICAN LIBRARY
TIMES MIRROR

PUBLISHER'S NOTE

This novel is a work of fiction. Names, characters, places, and incidents are either the product of the author's imagination or are used fictitiously, and any resemblance to actual persons, living or dead, events, or locales is entirely coincidental.

NAL BOOKS ARE AVAILABLE AT QUANTITY DISCOUNTS WHEN USED TO PROMOTE PRODUCTS OR SERVICES. FOR INFORMATION PLEASE WRITE TO PREMIUM MARKETING DIVISION, THE NEW AMERICAN LIBRARY, INC., 1633 BROADWAY, NEW YORK, NEW YORK 10019.

Copyright © 1980 by Sandra Heath

All rights reserved

SIGNET TRADEMARK REG. U.S. PAT. OFF. AND FOREIGN COUNTRIES
REGISTERED TRADEMARK—MARCA REGISTRADA
HECHO EN CHICAGO, U.S.A.

SIGNET, SIGNET CLASSICS, MENTOR, PLUME, MERIDIAN AND NAL BOOKS are published by The New American Library, Inc., 1633 Broadway, New York, New York 10019

First Printing, August, 1980

1 2 3 4 5 6 7 8 9

PRINTED IN THE UNITED STATES OF AMERICA

Chapter 1

The London streets were quiet in the October dawn. A thin mist clung to the ground, drifting between the trees in the square, and ghostly seagulls moved on the wet grass as a solitary carriage came slowly past the silent houses. The wheels rattled on the cobbles and the team moved at little more than a snail's pace.

Mally's head lolled on Chris's shoulder, the gentle motion of the carriage soothing her almost to the edge of sleep. Suddenly and without warning the carriage lurched to a standstill, the team rearing and plunging. Mally was brought to frightened awareness in a moment, her heart thundering as she heard the coachman's loud shout. The gray dawn was suddenly menacing, where a moment before it had been drowsy, and she clutched Chris's arm, her fingers digging through the costly black velvet.

He opened the door, leaning out. "What is it?"

"A man hiding in the trees, Sir Christopher," shouted the footman as he jumped down from the back of the carriage to come to the door. As he finished speaking, the ensuing silence was broken by the sound of running footsteps, dwindling away into the emptiness around them. The team was quiet now that the danger had gone.

Chris nodded at the footman. "Don't drive on just yet."

"Sir Christopher." The man bowed and pushed the door to.

Mally closed her eyes, leaning weakly back against the rich upholstery, and Chris turned to her, smoothing away a stray curl which rested against her cheek. "It's all right now, sweetheart, he's gone."

"I thought— Oh, Chris, for a moment I thought about Mrs. Harmon's murder!"

"That was in Llanglyn, not here in London."

"I cannot help it, Chris. I'd known her for so long and she was Mother's closest friend—a more sweet and gentle old lady you could not wish to meet."

"Tell me about it then, perhaps it will help."

She smiled at him. "It's merely my far-too-active-and-vivid imagination, I realize that, but I've had several letters from Mother. They're unhappy, frightened letters which have worried me so much that, like her, I'm jumping at every shadow. It happened about a month ago, I suppose. Someone broke into Mrs. Harmon's house in Llanglyn, brutally murdered her in her bed, and stole her jewelry—she was very rich, you know. A bit eccentric too, living alone in a small house in Breconshire when she could have afforded something as grand as your ancestral home. But she was a dear, and I loved her as if she were my aunt. To think that anyone could so cruelly murder her—" She stared at the cold, pale square, and it seemed for a moment that she could still hear those fleeing footsteps.

Chris kissed her cheek. "Don't think about it anymore."

"I cannot help it, for they haven't caught the murderer yet."

"And you think the fellow who just fled is the murderer

all the way from Llanglyn?" His voice was warm with fond humor as he smiled at her.

"Don't laugh."

"My sweet love, I have kept you up far too late and you are tired. Anyway, be logical—what have you got hidden away which is valuable enough to lure such a fiend? Mm?"

"Nothing to compare with Mrs. Harmon's diamonds, I suppose."

"Well then, end of conversation, I fancy, eh? And on to more pleasant things. I enjoyed myself tonight. When old Dansford throws an evening it takes me fully a week to recover! An oyster feast on the eve of St. Denys indeed! Still, it's as good a reason as any to make merry, I suppose." He leaned to tap the grille with his ivory-handled cane and the coach lurched on its way around the square.

Mally took a long breath. She must take Chris's advice and stop being foolish about the murder. *A pox on Mother for writing such hysterical letters*— She smiled. "Mr. Dansford keeps an almanac of reasons for each day of the year. And anyway, what's all this *fully a week to recover? You?* Sir Christopher Carlyon, you look fit to dance a good few measures yet, *and* consume even more maraschino."

"I intended enjoying myself on our first appearance in society since you accepted me, and enjoy myself I damned well did! How Dansford managed to assemble so many fashionable souls out of season amazes me."

"You make them sound like strawberries. Anyway, they came to cast their eyes over me, the woman who has finally trapped the Carlyon fortune in marriage—well, almost marriage, anyway. I shall never go to see a fairground monstrosity again, for now I know how they feel. One more raised lorgnette and I would have screamed!" The menace was slipping away slowly, and the uneasy rushing of her heart was gradually becoming calmer. The trees were just trees again—

"You enjoyed each close inspection, and don't pretend you didn't." He ran his fingers over her dark curls. "As I did myself. I paraded my triumph in grand style."

"*I'm* not a great catch, Chris. Now, if you had chosen Annabel—"

"I didn't want Annabel, earl's daughter or not. I've wanted you since the first time I saw you. And I *mean* the first time."

"I know," she whispered, slipping her fingers over his.

"You've taken some winning." He pulled her into his arms and kissed her.

He smiled. "I think Annabel could have kicked you for looking so magnificent tonight."

"And *I* could have kicked *you!*"

"Me? Why?"

"For being so unreasonably cool and abrupt with her. You had little cause to be quite so unpleasant, for she loves you a great deal still."

"Which is why I did it. I have now made it perfectly clear to her, haven't I?"

"Oh, perfectly. And unkindly."

"Are you going to be a nag, Marigold St. Aubrey? Because if you are, perhaps I should rush back to Annabel and grovel at her feet—"

She laughed. "I am not a nag, and I know full well how to be a perfect and loving wife." Even as the words were uttered she knew she had made a mistake. She felt him stiffen, and his smile faded as he removed his arm from her shoulders. The dawn, for a second time, was an unhappy place—

"We are almost there," he said curtly, "at Vimiero House."

"You don't have to say it like that."

"Don't I? You amaze me with your apparent unawareness of how your behavior can hurt. It's two years since Daniel died—*two years*—and yet only last week you caused the name of the house to be changed. I need no reminding that you were his wife, do I? Damn it all, he was my closest friend, but there are times now when I despise even the mention of his name!"

"That is a terrible thing to say."

"I will gladly say it again."

She twisted the strings of her reticule. Always, always it ended like this— "Chris, I didn't mean to hurt you."

"You never do, but still it happens time and time again. How do you really imagine I feel about this business of the house, eh? Well?" His soft brown eyes rested on her face.

She stared at the fine features which drew half the beauties in England like pins to a magnet. "Chris—"

"You aren't going to answer me, are you?"

"Is it so very reprehensible to carry out Daniel's last wish?"

"Reprehensible? No. Thoughtless. Pointless. Those words seem better suited to the occasion."

She bit back the anger he was rousing. "Daniel was proud of his part in the victory at Vimiero, and until his diary was sent to me a week or so ago I had no idea how much it meant to him. Chris, it took him nearly two months to die of his wounds, and the very last thing he ever wrote before he grew too weak was a scribbled line about changing the name of the house. You may call it thoughtless and pointless if you so desire—that is your privilege—but to me it is important."

"Oh, God, Mally, you're *still* his wife, aren't you? You're not my fiancée at all." He took her hands tightly. "I love you and have done since he first introduced his new bride to me that night eleven years ago, but for all that I've managed to achieve with you since his death, he might as well be still alive."

She drew her hands away. "I cannot and will not forget him."

"Have you even tried?"

"That was spiteful and childish!"

He ran his fingers through his light brown hair. "Childish? If wanting the love of the woman I am to marry is childish, then so be it."

She was shaking as she sat stiffly beside him, and the tears were very close as she slipped her hand into his, her ring catching in the lace spilling from beneath his cuff. "Chris," she whispered, "I'm sorry—"

His fingers tightened over hers immediately. "You could have confided in me about the house, couldn't you? Time and time again you keep me out of things, when you should share more. Silly things, like the business of Mrs. Harmon's murder. I had no idea it had upset you so much, you locked me out even from that."

"It seemed so foolish, to let something which happened the other side of the country frighten me so much. And as to the name of the house, I did not think it mattered."

"Oh, yes you did. You *knew* it mattered. But, as always, you put Daniel St. Aubrey first. No, don't snatch your hand away again, for these things should be aired between us." He gently touched her face. "I love you very dearly, Mally, and I need you to love me."

"I do, you must know that I do. But I cannot behave as if Daniel never existed. I am twenty-eight years old now and for most of my life I knew him, we even grew up together in the same house in Llanglyn. It's impossible for me never to mention him."

The carriage came to a standstill at last, outside her house, and it seemed to Mally that the mist deliberately swirled to reveal the new name. *Vimiero*. But it was 1810 now, not 1808. And there was Chris Carlyon. Not Daniel.

He raised her hand to his lips. "My love makes me unreasonable. Forgive me."

"I should have told you about the diary, I know that I should. I never mean to hurt you."

"And I never mean to be the original bear." He smiled.

She returned the smile. "I still feel foolish for telling you about the murder like that. It was more the behavior of a fifteen-year-old than a full-grown woman." She looked at the swirling mist, and tendrils of that earlier fear began to creep over her again, making her shiver in spite of her determination.

Chris tapped the grille again and the footman jumped down to open the door. "If I don't get you back to the nest, I shall run the risk of old Lucy taking a broom to my fashionable hide."

The cold air swept over them as he helped her down. The chandeliers in the vestibule threw jewel colors through the stained glass beside the doors. He wrapped her shawl around her as they climbed the steps to stand by the front doors, and they were both aware of the coachman staring so pointedly at his team and of the seemingly blind footman.

"Until tomorrow then, Mally," he whispered, kissing her hand.

"Don't you mean today?"

"Until later then."

The butler opened the doors and the light flooded out, making Chris's black velvet coat and lace-trimmed evening shirt look startling in the sudden glare. She stood by the doors as he returned to the carriage.

The perfectly matched roans pulled the heavy coach away into the mist, disturbing the restless seagulls so that they rose in a clamor from the grass. Their screams swung around the silent houses and somewhere close by a dog began to bark. Mally's eyes went immediately in the direction of that last sound, searching the shadows by the trees. But there was nothing there—

Digby closed the doors firmly on the cold autumn. "I

trust that you had an enjoyable time, madam," he said as he removed her shawl.

"Yes, thank you, Digby."

"Mrs. Berrisford is here, madam."

She stared, her heart sinking. "My mother? All the way from Breconshire without so much as a note to tell me she was coming? Is something wrong?"

"Well, madam, I would hazard a guess that she is worried about something, but more than that I cannot say."

"It's probably her nerves since poor Mrs. Harmon was murdered. Is my sister with her?" The words sounded lame as she tried not to show how disturbed she felt.

"No, madam, Miss Maria did not come."

She smiled. "No, Maria's nerves are as steady as a rock. Did you put Mother in the Green Room?"

"Yes, madam. Lucy informs me that she believes her to be sleeping now."

"Believes?"

"Mrs. Berrisford has locked herself in, madam."

"Then—then I will not disturb her. Good night, Digby."

"Good night, madam."

She crossed the polished tiles of the hall and wearily climbed the curving staircase. She paused by the oil lamp in its silver-gilt holder, looking across the stairwell at Daniel's prized collection of Stubbs's paintings. They were surely not valuable enough— Taking a long, cross breath, she continued up the stairs. At the first landing she halted again, looking back down at the paintings which Daniel had collected so painstakingly. Was Chris right? *Did* she still put Daniel first—even now? Slowly, and with a heavy heart, she went on up toward the second floor, and as she reached her own rooms she heard the clock of St. Blaise's strike four o'clock.

Chapter 2

Lucy drew the rose brocade chair before the fire and ushered Mally firmly into it. "Sit down there in the warm while I make you a nightcap."

"If I drink anything more I shall have the head to end all heads in the morning."

"Just warm milk then."

Mally nodded, wriggling her feet from the velvet slippers. She stretched her toes toward the fire and stared at the slow, curling flames. Without Lucy's presence the room was so quiet, and beyond the drawn curtains she could still hear the seagulls. And the dog. But in the warm safety of her room the unreasonable fear could not reach her in the same way, and as she stared at the glow in the heart of the fire, it was of Chris that she thought.

Lucy returned with the glass of milk and stood watching her sadly. Lucy had looked after Mally since childhood, and there was nothing which the old nurse did not know. "How did it go, sweeting?"

"Terribly."

Lucy's crisply starched apron crackled as she crouched

beside the chair and took Mally's hand. "There now, don't fret about it."

"I can't help it. Every time it happens. Every single time. It always comes back to Daniel."

"Sir Christopher should be man enough to understand."

Mally looked fondly at the nurse's old face framed by its mobcap and wispy strands of gray hair. "But he doesn't understand, Lucy, he thinks I'm—dwelling. And perhaps he's right, for it's two long years now. Two very long years."

"I know, and it's autumn again."

"That doesn't help. It's worse when the fires are lit again, and then when the chrysanthemums are brought in— It's the chrysanthemums more than anything." She stared at the fire again. "They were by his bed the day he died."

"But there will always be autumns, and always chrysanthemums, little one. You must go on, you cannot keep looking back at what you have lost."

"I know, I am unfair to you all. To you. Even to poor old Digby. And most of all to Chris—he deserves more than me, Lucy."

Lucy smiled and patted the gloved hand. "But it's you that he wants, Miss Mall."

"Lucy, you loved your husband Joseph, didn't you? How long does it take to forget?"

"Forget? Lord above, you don't *forget!* Memories mellow, but they don't suddenly vanish like will-o'-the-wisp. Even now, eighteen years after he was taken from me, I— Well, you have your autumns, but for me it is the springtime. When the daffodils are there again. Joseph was the head gardener up at Castell Melyn when I first met him. Oh, it was a grand place then, with all the carriages, the fine folk, the lights and the music. You've not seen the old place like that, have you? To you it's always been gloomy and deserted, a place for children to avoid because the ghosts await them. But in the spring the daffodils must still be there, where my Joseph first planted them. I've never been back since he died, but in my mind's eye I can imagine them. Drift after drift of pale gold, and beyond that the castle itself with the sun on its yellow stone. Castell Melyn. Whatever knight in times gone by named it that named it well, for it is truly a yellow castle. An enchanted place for me, a frightening place for you." Lucy smiled. "I've heard tell recently, mind, that someone's bought it and it's lived in again. Perhaps it will come into its own again, eh, Miss Mall?"

"I haven't been near the place since that time Daniel locked me in somewhere there and wouldn't let me out."

"Aye, and a good thrashing he got from his father on account of it. That wasn't long before his parents were taken by the smallpox. His parents. Your uncle. And half the folk of Llanglyn. So Daniel came to live beneath the same roof as you, and that was the beginning of it, wasn't it?"

Mally nodded. "Maria got so jealous and furious because we wouldn't play with her. We'd go sneaking off, hoping that she hadn't seen us. But she usually found us in the end, and spoiled all our games by insisting on having everything her own way. Poor Maria." Mally finished the milk. "Lucy—why is Mother here?"

"I don't know." Lucy got to her feet.

"Didn't she say anything to you?"

"No."

Mally glanced at the curtained windows. "She must have said something."

"Only when I asked her if they'd caught the murderer. She looked fit to burst into tears and said that they hadn't. Then she went and locked herself in the Green Room."

"I know, Digby told me."

"She's very upset about it," said Lucy heavily, "as I am myself. And as you are too, if I'm not mistaken."

"Don't you miss anything?"

"Not where my lamb is concerned. I've seen you jump when a door banged, and glance over your shoulder where the shadows are darker. And it's only since the murder."

"I know, and I'm disgusted with myself for giving in like this. Oh, I *wish* Mother had let us know she was coming, for she's managed to unsettle me all over again now."

"Well, you know your mam, Miss Mall, she's a creature of impulse if ever I knew one." Lucy smiled reassuringly. "My, your hair stayed in a treat tonight. I'll warrant Sir Christopher was the proudest man there."

"It went very well until the usual subject cropped up on the way home. It was the naming of the house this time."

"Well, sweeting, you *were* a little tactless there, weren't you?"

"I know. Lucy, do you like him?"

"Sir Christopher? But of course I do, I like him very much." Lucy unpinned the intricate curls and dropped the pins into a porcelain dish. "But perhaps he's not for you."

"Why do you say that?"

"Because it seems to my old eyes that he wants a blushing bride who behaves like a maid in the midst of her first love. If that is what he wants, then he shouldn't be marrying the widow of his best friend, now should he?"

Mally looked at the emerald ring on her finger, turning it so that the flames caught it in flashes of deep green. "I love him."

"I know you do, but do you love him enough and in the right way?"

Mally removed the ring and pulled off her white eve-

ning gloves. The ring felt cold when at last she replaced it.
"I want to marry him, Lucy."

"Then carry on as you now do, biting back each unwary word, concealing the truth of how you feel deep inside, and enduring his behavior when he senses you are not being honest with him."

"You make it sound like a life sentence, not marriage."

Lucy glanced down at her and said nothing, picking up the hairbrush and brushing the dark hair until it crackled.

When at last Mally was ready to climb into the warmed bed with its lavender-scented sheets, the dawn had turned from gray to silver outside. She lay back, watching Lucy draw the heavy velvet curtains around the bed.

"I wonder if someone *has* bought Castell Melyn? Would you go there again if they had? In the springtime?"

Lucy smiled fondly. "Perhaps. Who can say? Now then, you get some sleep. Good night, Miss Mall."

"Good night."

The last curtain shut out the light completely, and Mally lay in the darkness. Outside the seagulls had gone and the dog had ceased its noise, and the only sound was the slow rattle and clatter of wheels upon the cobbles as a tradesman's cart passed the house.

Chapter 3

It was the sun managing to pierce its way through a crack in the curtains which woke her at last the next morning. The clock of St. Blaise's was just striking and she lay there counting the chimes. Nine. Ten. Eleven. Eleven o'clock!

"Lucy?"

"I'm here, just warming your wrap. It's a grand morning, cold, but sunny and fine."

"And Mother will no doubt have been up for hours!"

"No. She has only just unlocked herself from her cell and gone downstairs. She told me that she had journeyed here in two days from Llanglyn and that she put her exceedingly long sleep down to that."

Mally smiled. "Not to mention the hidden bottle of something or other she carries around in that huge reticule! Purely medicinal, of course."

"Miss Mall, perhaps I should warn you."

Mally paused on the edge of the bed. "What?"

"Well, I don't think Mrs. Berrisford has come here just because of what happened to Mrs. Harmon. I think she's very worried about something else."

"Why do you think that?"

"My room is above the Green Room, and I couldn't help— Well, I couldn't help hearing her last night. She was crying, Miss Mall, and I don't think worrying about Mrs. Harmon's death would cause that. Do you?"

"Maybe not." Mally slipped her arms into the warmed wrap. "I'll go down directly then. Just brush my hair and tie it back. That's it."

"What clothes should I set out for you afterwards?"

"The blue and white dimity, I think. Yes, Sir Christopher is taking me for a drive in Hyde Park this afternoon and the blue and white will look well. Could you have them prepare a hot bath for me in about an hour's time? Good and hot, scented with something flowery and at the very least up to my chin! That will set me up for the rest of the day, and I fancy that after my breakfast with Mother I shall need setting up again."

The fresh bowls of chrysanthemums on the polished table were bright rust and gold in the sunlight streaming through the dining-room window, and their wistful, clean scent filled the air as Mally entered the room. She glanced at them immediately and then at the plump little figure in apple green silk by the windows.

Mrs. Berrisford's hands twisted and twisted the lace handkerchief she held and she stared out at the mass of Michaelmas daisies lining the sun-drenched wall of the garden. Some late roses bobbed here and there, but the Michaelmas daisies were in tumbling confusion everywhere this autumn, a blaze of purple and pink against the mellow brick.

Digby drew back Mally's chair and she met his glance, nodding at him. "Leave us, I think, Digby, and thank you."

He bowed and Mrs. Berrisford turned at last as the doors closed behind him. "Ah, Marigold."

Mally smiled, but mentally gritted her teeth, for her name was the one thing in the whole world she hated. "How good it is to see you, Mother." She crossed the remaining space and hugged her mother's dumpy figure.

"I must ask you, Marigold, for I cannot contain myself a moment longer. Have you seen Maria?"

"Maria? No."

"Oh, dear, I hoped and hoped— I wrote those letters, praying that by some phrase you would hint you had seen her." Her eyes filled with tears and she shook from head to toe.

So that was behind the letters— "Come and sit down, Mother," said Mally gently, leading the quivering woman toward the fire and sitting her firmly in the large armchair. "Now then, what's all this about?"

"W-well, I haven't seen her for three weeks or more." Mrs. Berrisford pushed her henna-rinsed wig more firmly beneath her lace mobcap. "I don't know why she should do this to me, especially at a time like this when we don't know if we're to be murdered in our beds!"

"What happened before she left?"

"Nothing." But Mally noticed how her mother avoided her eyes.

"Mother, has she gone to the Clevelys?"

"I don't know. Oh, Marigold, do be sensible, how can I go there and ask that old dragon if my daughter happens to have gone to stay there? She'd have the engagement to her precious Thomas broken off quicker than a wink! She doesn't approve of Maria anyway, the world and his wife knows that, and an inquiry like that would only convince her further that Maria is unsuitable. With a capital U."

"Well, is the admirable Thomas in residence at the moment?"

"No, he's at sea—in more ways than one!"

Mally smiled in spite of her mother's worried face. "But why did you think she'd come here?"

Again there was that refusal to meet her daughter's eyes. "Because—she took the royal mail at Hereford. She bought a ticket for London. I thought—hoped—that she had come to you. We, well, you see, we had had some terrible disagreements."

"About Thomas Clevely?"

"Good heavens, no! What could you find to talk about in *him!* He'll make a wealthy husband. End of topic. No, no, it was about—someone else."

"Another man?"

Mrs. Berrisford shifted uncomfortably in her seat. "Yes, but it's not quite that simple. There *was* another man, a totally disreputable American by the name of Andrew York. A ruffian and a scoundrel. Just like his master."

Mally blinked. "Who is or was this Andrew York? I mean, where does he live?"

"He lived at Castell Melyn. He came with *that man.*"

"What man? Oh, Mother, you are leaving me floundering around in all these dark utterances and I haven't the slightest idea what you are talking about. Now then, Maria was seeing this Andrew York from Castell Melyn, is that right?"

"Yes. Foolish chit. She was jeopardizing a perfectly good match and I told her so. In fact I forbade her to see Mr. York again. Oh, I was most forcible, I may tell you." Mrs. Berrisford nodded firmly.

"And?"

"And she continued to see him. Behind my back. It came to a head on the night poor dear Agatha was murdered. I could not find Maria anywhere. I was frantic because it was such a stormy night. The old oak up at the crossroads was brought down. Oh, *such* a gale. Then Maria came home. It was so late and I was nearly fainting with the worry of it all. She was so pale, like death itself, and she wouldn't tell me anything, just shut herself in her room. The next morning, of course, the news was everywhere about the murder. I thought—well, because she was so strange, I thought perhaps she had seen something in the town. I know that she had gone to Llanglyn to meet the American. I asked her, but she just burst into tears. Pattie and I could do nothing with her. Then Dr. Towers came to the house. He'd been up at Castell Melyn attending that Negro everyone *knows* now did the murder but who's being protected by the doctor's insistence that he was too ill to have left his bed!"

"Mother, you're losing me again. What happened when Dr. Towers came to the house?"

"He asked to see Maria and was closeted with her in the library for some time. Well, whatever it was he had to say, it brought a change in her. She seemed lighter when he had gone, but she was still strange and withdrawn and would say nothing to me. Even Pattie tried—now you know Pattie's kept house for us for years and years and Maria always confided in her, but no, not this time." Mrs. Berrisford drew a long, shaking breath. "Next morning she had gone. She packed a small handcase of belongings and just left the house."

"To go to this Andrew York?"

"If she did, then her journey was in vain, for Mr. York was dead. The day Maria left, his body was found up near the castle. A riding mishap, it seems. Dr. Towers told me he was found with his foot still caught in the stirrup. He'd been dragged some way, poor man. Anyway, he's buried at St. Crispin's now, God rest his soul. And there's still no sign of Maria. If you ask me, that Negro murdered Agatha *and* Mr. York!"

"Mother!"

"Well, Marigold, he *was* in Llanglyn that night. He was seen. And nothing that old fool Towers says can alter that."

"Who saw him?"

"Jasper Turney and his brother. And Brew Darril."

"Three of the biggest rogues I've ever clapped eyes on! Shame on you for putting their word above the doctor's."

"Hereford born and bred, the three of them—so what can you expect but that they're rogues." Mrs. Berrisford sniffed. "Anyway, Marigold, it isn't only their word. Pattie saw the Negro as well, in the lane by our house. So, you see, the doctor is fibbing—the Negro was *not* too ill to move."

Mally sighed. "What was Andrew York like?"

Her mother shrugged. "Good-looking, I suppose. He had a sort of lost look, almost like a little boy, if that doesn't sound too ridiculous. He perfectly *devastated* Maria."

What had happened in Llanglyn that night? Mally stood by the window. And why had Maria disappeared? She cannot have gone with Andrew York. Nor can she have gone to the boring Thomas Clevely. But she had stopped to pack a handcase and had taken a ticket for London.

"Mother, I must ask this. What sort of an association did Maria have with Andrew York?"

"Marigold!"

"Well, it must be asked, mustn't it?"

"María was not *enceinte!*"

"Can you know that for certain?"

Mrs. Berrisford lowered her eyes sadly. "I cannot," she whispered.

"So, it *is* possible?"

"Anything is possible, Marigold. And—"

"Yes?"

"And she *was* besotted with him. She loved him most foolishly, and—yes, perhaps sufficiently to throw caution to the winds. Oh, dear, if only she would just return, I would forgive her anything just to know that she is safe and well."

"Did you find out if she actually got on the mail?"

"Yes. She did."

Mally smiled. "Then she must be all right if she got as far as Hereford and the mail coach. She is up here somewhere, presumably. But why did she not come to me?" Mally stood, and going to the table, poured two cups of coffee from the silver pot. The toast was cold now as she scraped some butter over it and then dipped the spoon into the cook's excellent lime marmalade. "Come and eat something, Mother, and we shall think of what we can do next. Have a cup of this good Turkish coffee to begin with."

"*Turkish?* Oh, my dear, I don't think—"

"Nonsense, you just taste it before you grizzle. Now then, do you know what Maria was wearing when she left?"

"Oh, dear, the man at the inn in Hereford *did* say. It was that little spencer, you know the one I mean, trimmed with white fur. A sort of donkey-brown velvet, I think you would describe it. And a cream-colored gown beneath. A straw bonnet."

"Donkey brown and cream. Not exactly likely to remain in anyone's memory, is it?" Mally nibbled the toast, staring out at the swaying Michaelmas daisies. "Mother, I think we shall have to send for Mr. Paulington."

"Who?"

"Mr. Paulington." Mally thought distastefully of the sly little man with the foxy face and dreadful tweed coat. "He—undertakes to make investigations for people, if you know what I mean."

"Indeed I do not! What sort of investigations?"

"Well, one of Daniel's friends thought his wife was being unfaithful to him and he came to Daniel with his suspicions. Daniel knew of this Mr. Paulington and gave his friend his address. And sure enough, within a week or so of having been hired, Mr. Paulington produced evidence of the wife's infidelities, the times, the places, and the names of the various gentlemen concerned."

"Good heavens, and *you* were present at such a conversation?"

"Yes."

"Oh, that was not admirable of dear late Daniel, not admirable at all. It was lax of him to allow you to remain in the room."

"Oh, Mother."

"And you think Mr. Paulington may be able to help us find Maria?"

"He can but try. And don't worry, if Maria took herself to London, then she cannot be another victim of this murderer Llanglyn seems to be harboring at the moment. I will send Digby this very day to Mr. Paulington's address."

Mally buttered another piece of toast. She had spoken a little more confidently than she felt about finding Maria. There were countless mails arriving at the Swan with Two Necks each day and countless passengers pouring in and out of each one. Would even the redoubtable Mr. Paulington be able to discover a forgotten memory at the back of someone's mind?

Chapter 4

Mally surveyed her reflection, tweaking and prinking the blue and white dimity.

Mrs. Berrisford watched her. "Good Heavens, Marigold, you will *crease* it by fiddling so! Surely Sir Christopher is not going to notice the *exact* hang of each fold!" She looked around the room. "You'll live in grand style soon, my dear. I hear tell that the Carlyon estates and house are absolutely beyond this world! *Absolutely!* And to think that my daughter has snapped him up. The Carlyon marriage. Oh, Llanglyn has rung with the news, I can tell you!"

The Carlyon marriage. "I am marrying him because I love him, not because he is a grand catch, Mother."

"Of course you are, my dear. But nonetheless you are *made. Made.*"

Mally picked up her bonnet and put it carefully over her piled curls.

Mrs. Berrisford picked up the engagement ring which Mally had placed on the dressing table. "Great happiness is granted to us all perhaps once, but you, my dear, seem especially fortunate to have it granted twice."

"Twice?" Mally stared at the ring. "Have I been granted that then?"

Mrs. Berrisford looked up. "Am I wrong then? Are you not as deeply in love with him as you have hitherto stated?"

"Of course I'm in love with him!"

"Don't snap my head off, my dear, I believe you. Still—not that it matters—he's got what he wanted and it's up to him now."

"There speaks a woman of the world?"

"No, Marigold, there speaks a member of the older generation. I happen to believe, rightly or wrongly, that it is still up to the *man* to make his wife happy. Not the other way around." Mrs. Berrisford stood and drew the lace curtains aside. "Ah, I thought I heard something. Sir Christopher is here, my dear."

Mally's heart lurched. Would it be all right this afternoon?

Chris bowed over Mally's hand and looked up in surprise as he saw Mrs. Berrisford.

"Why, Mally, I had no idea your mother was visiting you at the moment."

Mrs. Berrisford threw a pleading look at her elder daughter. Mally smiled at him. "She—she has been upset by the murder of her old friend, Mrs. Agatha Harmon, Chris, and she has come to spend a few days with me to get over it."

He was concerned immediately, taking Mrs. Berrisford's hand. "I had not realized. But we must do what we can to take your mind off so sad a matter. I shall see to it that your time here is gay and enjoyable, Mrs. Berrisford."

She flushed uncomfortably. "Oh, please, Sir Christopher, do not concern yourself with me."

"And why not?" he said with a smile. Mally watched him. He could surely charm any bird off any tree—

Mrs. Berrisford went pink with pleasure. "Because I am an old biddy who has no wish to play gooseberry to you and Marigold."

"If you join us in Hyde Park this afternoon it could be that the crush will place us next to an eligible earl," he teased.

"I do not want an eligible earl, thank you very much." She tapped his arm with her closed fan, "But thank you for your concern. I shall remain here and chitter-chatter with Lucy."

She watched him as he picked up his top hat and gloves. He was surely the very picture of everything elegant and fashionable. There was an air of endless quality about Sir Christopher Carlyon, from the full muslin cravat and frilled shirt, to the dull gray coat and brocade waistcoat. A peacock-colored waistcoat, but so perfect. Mrs. Berrisford sighed with satisfaction. Just wait until that sour old Mrs. Clevely saw Marigold walk up the aisle with such a prize! Just wait! Look down her nose at Maria then, would she? Mrs. Berrisford gloated over the forthcoming sweet satisfaction of glorying over the opposition. She studied him again as he handed Mally her gloves. So slender and fine in these new fashions the gentlemen wore these days. Her smile faltered a little as she glanced down at his tight-fitting cream-colored trousers. That was perhaps a fashion she couldn't approve of, revealing as it did things which were better not revealed! But still, if a man had the figure to follow such a fashion, then she supposed he was well advised to do just that—for the Lord alone knew what the next foible of the *haut ton* would be—crimson thigh boots and sailors' hats, no doubt—

The crush in Hyde Park was one of the worst Mally could remember. The last one to compare had been on that rainy day when she and Daniel had driven out in the barouche and the axle had broken, causing the very devil of a jam. She smiled to herself, glancing at Chris—but she could not mention that day to him, could she? Not even as an amusing memory.

She slipped her hand in his and he smiled at her. Just then the carriage come to a standstill and a man on a nervous black horse reined in beside them.

Chris leaned forward suddenly, opening the carriage door. "Richard! Richard Vallender! You old stoat, where've you been all these years?"

The other turned at the remembered voice and his thin, dark face broke into a grin. "Chris! It takes a jam in Hyde Park to find you again! You're getting fat with soft living!" He maneuvered his horse closer, his thin body moving as one with the animal.

Chris laughed. "Fat? Well, we can't all be human beansticks, can we? Where've you been hiding?"

"Here and there."

"Mostly there, no doubt."

Richard dismounted and soothed his anxious mount, his glance falling on Mally for the first time. "Won't you introduce me, Chris? Or are you afraid I'll snatch her from under your very nose?" He took off his top hat, revealing a mass of thick dark wavy hair.

Chris raised his eyebrow. "Me? Afraid of your prowess in that direction! That will surely be the day the heavens really do rain cats and dogs! Richard, allow me to introduce my fiancée, Mrs. St. Aubrey. Mally, Richard Vallender, of ill repute."

Richard's eyes swung to her as he heard her name. "St. Aubrey? Not—?"

Chris nodded. "Daniel's widow, Richard."

"But I had no idea he was dead, nor indeed that he

had married! Forgive me, Mrs. St. Aubrey, but what happened?"

She glanced unhappily at Chris, but surely this was none of her fault, this twist of the conversation? "Mr. Vallender, Daniel was wounded at Vimiero two years ago and died of those wounds."

Chris still held her hand. "Richard, you left our circle a long time ago indeed—even I had forgotten it was that long!"

Richard grinned. "A mere lad I was, and all innocence."

"In a pig's eye!" Chris pushed his shoulder fondly.

Richard took Mally's other hand and raised it to his lips. "I take my hat off to you, madam, for to have nailed Chris's hide to the wall is quite an achievement."

Chris sat back. "Take your lecherous eyes away, Richard, for she's mine—you must find your own lady. Unless, of course, you already have."

Richard's smile faded. "I did, Chris, I did. But she died."

"I'm sorry, Richard, truly I am."

The quicksilver smile was there again as Richard tapped his hat back on his head again. "Well, Mrs. St. Aubrey, you and I may commiserate, may we not? That will surely drive Chris here to distraction, for he does fear my spellbinding charm with the fair sex, no matter what he may say to the contrary!"

She smiled, but was glad as he remounted his restless horse. Had she engineered it the conversation could not have taken a more delicate turn.

Chris looked up at him. "Where *have* you been anyway?"

"America. But I am back for good now. As a matter of fact, Mrs. St. Aubrey, I am back in Daniel's neck of the woods. Llanglyn."

She stared at him. "Does Llanglyn know?" she asked with a laugh.

"Oh, yes. It is perfectly well aware of me, I do assure you!" He smiled at her, but a strange expression passed through his dark eyes. "It was a coincidence really. I intended coming back to England when Gillian died, there seemed no reason to stay over there. I picked up a journal in New York, in a hotel smoking room. And there it was. An advertisement for a castle in Wales, and in a town I had actually heard of, having known Daniel came from there."

Her eyes widened. "So *you* are the new owner of Castell Melyn?"

"I have that honor. But I suppose, being Daniel's wife, you would be bound to have heard of it, wouldn't you?"

"Mr. Vallender, I was born and brought up in Llanglyn too. But surely there is much needed to be done to the castle to make it habitable?"

"Enough." He nodded. "Enough indeed. But it's done now and I'm penniless again. You must come and visit my new domain. I have always wanted to behave like a medieval baron and have feasts in a great hall."

Chris laughed. "And toss bones to the hounds on the rushes?"

"Something like that. Baron Vallender of Castell Melyn. I have a notion for a title." Richard looked at Mally again. "You must come to the castle, Mrs. St. Aubrey, and see for yourself how excellently it has been done up."

"If Chris agrees, then of course I'd be delighted to come." She smiled at him, liking him for his impetuosity.

"Chris?" Richard grinned wickedly. "Oh, him—yes, I suppose he'll have to be included, won't he?"

Chris leaned out to close the door as the crush began to sort itself out. "Old Nick is alive and well—and living in Llanglyn!"

Richard soothed the restless horse again. "Alive and well and impoverished. Where shall I find you, Chris?"

"Pendleton Square. Number four."

"Nob territory. Will I be shot on sight?"

"No, you're not in season. Call on me, Richard."

"I will, you may depend upon it. Good day to you, Mrs. St. Aubrey."

Chris closed the door as the carriage began to move, and already Richard Vallender had passed from sight ahead of them. "Mally, I never thought I would see him again."

"How did you meet?"

"On our respective Grand Tours. We all stayed in the same establishment in Venice. Oh, and a fine time was had by one and all. Daniel nearly drowned in the Grand Canal, Richard floated away in a gondola leaving the pole stuck in the mud, and I stood on the bridge helpless with laughter!" He smiled. "We attended Eton together and then somehow Richard was parted from us. I only thought of him the other day." He tilted her face toward his. "He was right, you know—he was always the very devil with the womenfolk. He'd give me a run for my money, I fancy."

"With *me?*" She smiled and kissed him. "I don't like human beansticks."

He looked beyond her to the other window of the carriage and grinned. "We are observed. Lady Annabel Murchison, no less. Don't you feel the daggers in your back?" He pulled her closer for Annabel's benefit. "Oh, how I enjoy being the object of such jealousy."

"You rat." She laughed, glancing behind at Annabel's crimson face.

"It does my male pride endless good. I'm dining with her father tonight, a small matter of a thousand of my acres he wants to buy. I'll see how high I can get him— he's dripping with money."

"So are you."

"That's the name of the game, sweetheart. I don't want anything of his, so I'm calling the tune. Did you notice that beast Richard was riding, to change the subject like the grasshopper I am?"

"Yes, I noticed it. Some sort of thoroughbred was about all I could say to describe it."

"Thoroughbred blood, undoubtedly. Rangy. It looked a good goer." He put his arm around her shoulder as the carriage swayed around a corner and out of the park. "I was thinking the other day that if there was one man in the world I would like for my best man, it would be Richard Vallender. Now he can be, eh?"

"But what of your brother Henry?"

"Henry can go whistle for the honor, I fear. I hadn't asked him anyway. He's still with the cavalry somewhere or other, cutting a dash if nothing else."

"You are cruel. Henry is a fine officer."

"With notions of grandeur. Sees himself as another budding Boney. Perhaps he is."

"Well, as Henry is a second son with little hope of inheriting when he has such a hale and healthy brother, I think he's doing very well."

"Aye," he agreed, "little brother Harry does well enough—not that I would let him know I think that, for there'd be no living with him."

She untied her bonnet and tossed it across to the other seat next to her reticule. "I wonder what your Mr. Vallender's wife was like?"

"If he intends commiserating with you, then you will no doubt find out."

She glanced at him quickly. "I'm sorry—" she began and felt immediately like biting her tongue off.

"Sorry? Why?"

"Nothing."

"Tell me."

"It was nothing, really."

He took a long breath. "Mally, what are you sorry about? God above, we are at it again! Why, oh *why*, won't you tell me things?"

She looked away. *Because when I do it's the wrong thing too*— "I was going to say that I was sorry the conversation went the way it did."

"Why should you apologize for that?"

"I don't really know." The words fell uneasily into the carriage.

The moments passed, and then he took her hand. "Perhaps we should get around to naming the day, eh? Perhaps that will solve our nit-picking?"

Suddenly the thought of actually having the day set was all wrong, not when they argued and misunderstood each other all the time— Her silence could not be mistaken.

Chris turned her face toward him. "The lack of sound is deafening. Don't you want to marry me?"

"Yes, yes, of course I do. But we should not argue so much and maybe marriage will not stop it. I didn't mean to make you think—"

"You—didn't—mean—to—make—me—think." He spaced the words slowly and deliberately. "Damn you, Mally! You *never* do, do you? But that does not stop you doing it time and time again! How ever you managed to make Daniel so perfect and exquisite a wife I'll never know, for if there is one thing you exceed at it's bringing a man so low that he could cheerfully cut his own throat as a blessed relief!"

She stared at him. "If that's how you truly feel—"

"Oh, it is!"

The carriage had slowed at a congested road junction and Mally did not stop to think. She flung open the door and jumped down onto the cobbles. The door swung behind her as she ran between the chaises and vans, a bright blue and white figure which startled some of the horses and caused a fruiterer's cart to almost overturn.

"Mally!"

She heard Chris calling her. She turned down an alley, pushing her way through the crowds and hurrying until she was sure he could not find her.

Chapter 5

It wasn't until the breeze tore at her carefully pinned hair that she realized she had left her bonnet in the carriage. To be seen walking without her bonnet— Still trembling and blinking back the tears, she stood outside a teashop, staring at the elegant dish of éclairs displayed in the window. The strains of music drifted out into the street from the small orchestra playing inside, and her spirits sank even lower as she sought her handkerchief— which was also still in the carriage. She glanced around. Where was she? She had come down the alleyway and into this street so swiftly and without paying attention, and now she really did not recognize anything around her. Or anyone.

She returned her attention to the éclairs, gazing at the thick cream and soft chocolate. At any other time she would have taken a delight in eating so fine a pastry, but today, when everything had gone so hopelessly wrong—

The reflection of a tall, golden-haired figure in dull green velvet appeared in the window beside her.

Annabel smiled at her. "Good afternoon, Mrs. St. Aubrey."

"Good afternoon, Lady Annabel."

The smile was there again, rather too sweetly for Mally's liking. "I was about to take some tea here, would you care to join me? I saw how you were admiring the éclairs and they are indeed most excellent. Please join me."

Mally could think of nothing to say, and she could not bring herself to be out-and-out rude by refusing. "I—"

"Oh, please do, unless of course you have an appointment." Annabel's eyes moved briefly to Mally's bare head.

"Thank you, Lady Annabel, I should like to join you."

The waitress placed the dish of cakes next to the silver teapot and bobbed a neat curtsey, smiling charmingly all the while.

Annabel leaned forward to Mally. "Most excellent service here. Small wonder that everyone who is anyone comes here after Hyde Park."

"Do they?" Mally glanced around. It was dark inside the tearooms, except for the small dais where the three-piece orchestra was playing. The tables were all prettily furnished with pink and white floral cloths and posies of late summer roses. And as she looked around she saw that she did indeed know quite a number of the people sitting at their tea.

Annabel watched her. "But of course everyone comes here, it's *the* thing this year. Petcholli's Tea Shop after the drive. Don't tell me you hadn't heard that."

"No, I hadn't."

"Chris is hiding you away too much. But where is he? He was with you in the park, was he not?"

Mally decided that the time for this cat-and-mouse game to end had most definitely arrived. "You know perfectly well that he was, Lady Annabel."

Again the smile. "I know—I was praying you would quarrel insurmountably. There, is that not honest of me?"

Mally was forced to smile. "Yes, it is, very honest."

"I make no secret of loving him still. I'd snatch him from under your nose in a trice if I could. *Have* you had an argument?"

"That is none of your business."

"That means you have."

Mally poured two cups of the weak tea. "I really don't know why I'm sitting here with you like this. Where is your chaperone?"

"Still in the barouche, I fancy. But as you are a respectable widow, you will pass excellently as a chaperone for a young, unmarried lady such as myself. Won't you?" Annabel's green eyes shone.

Mally put down her cup. "Still in the barouche. You *saw* me flounce from the carriage, didn't you?"

"Yes."

"I should have known you'd still be spying."

Annabel looked angelic. "Actually I wasn't. It was the wildly banging carriage door, the flash of your bare head passing my window, and the shouting and fist-waving of the other drivers which alerted me."

"I know, I *did* make a solomon of it, didn't I?" Mally nodded ruefully. "And you, Lady Annabel Murchison, are the last person I should talk of it with, as you are my arch rival."

"I must correct that statement. "I am the *would be* arch rival, but I don't get much of a look-in, do I? I have always been second best, but I can live with it. I think."

"You must love him a great deal, Lady Annabel."

"I do. May I call you Mally again? We were friends once."

"And let a snake in the grass wriggle even closer to me?"

"Why not? It will keep you on your toes."

"And wear me out with anxiety as to what you were up to."

"Ah, but you'll have to worry about that anyway, won't you? I have decided, you see, that I must make one last despairing bid to get him back."

"Is this the gauntlet on the ground?" asked Mally, sitting back.

"Well"—Annabel smiled—"I could not respect myself if I let him slip away without at least trying, could I?"

Mally raised her eyebrows. "Try away then, Annabel."

"Eat your éclair. They *are* good, you know."

"And just how well do you know the proprietors of this establishment? Well enough to have this éclair laced with something final?"

"Oh, that wouldn't be the thing. For my own pride and self-respect I have to *win* him from you. So your heroine's death among the chocolate and cream would do my cause little good, wouldn't it?"

"After that I think I *will* eat this confection then."

Annabel drank her tea. "You know, Mally, I rather like you. Damn you. What *did* you quarrel about?"

"Mind your own business."

"I can guess anyway."

"How?" Mally licked her fingertips.

"It can only be the one thing, the only thing ever to screw Chris up to a pitch."

Mally flushed. "And that might be—?"

"Daniel St. Aubrey, of course."

"This is delicate ground, Annabel, and definitely not ground I wish to tread with you."

"You're blushing, Mally."

"So would you be. Please, Annabel, leave it alone." Mally looked steadily at the golden-haired girl.

"I did not realize the wound was still so open, Mally. I'm sorry."

They fell silent for a moment and then Mally cast around for her reticule, forgetting again that she did not have it with her. "I must be getting back, my mother will be wondering where I am."

"Shall we share a chaise? After all, we live in the same square, do we not?"

Mally just wished to get away from her enforced companion. "I think I will go alone, Annabel."

"Then you will have a long walk, I fear. And my reputation may suffer a little from being unescorted."

Mally sighed. The reticule.

Annabel smiled. "The offer of a shared chaise is still there. Oh, come on, I'm not poisonous—not really anyway."

Mally laughed defeatedly. "That sounds like the understatement of the century!"

The chaise rocked and bumped down Pall Mall and Mally gripped the handrail, wincing with each lurch. "Good heavens, I had no idea traveling could be so uncomfortable still."

"Soft living," replied Annabel.

"That's the second time this afternoon I've heard that phrase."

"Oh? Who else said it then?"

"Not Chris, if that's what you're fishing for. No, it was one Richard Vallender, widower, of Breconshire. Now *there's* a handsome, winning gentleman for you, Annabel, wickedly charming and looking for a second wife."

"I'm not sniffing the market for husbands, I'll have you know."

"No, but your snout is a little too close to my corner of the yard."

Annabel laughed. "Not really, I don't stand an earthly."

"I wouldn't be so sure. After today's episode I think my stock is rather low *chez* Carlyon."

"You cannot mean that."

Mally said nothing as the chaise wobbled around yet another corner. She heard the comforting sound of a familiar clock, St. Blaise's. The driver flicked his whip at the weary horse and it moved a little more swiftly, setting the unsteady remains of the springs heaving from side to side again. Annabel gripped the door handle for support, glancing suddenly at Mally as she saw Chris's carriage drawn up outside Vimiero House.

As the chaise ground to a standstill, Chris was just coming down the white steps. Mally climbed down with Annabel, who was determined not to drive on around to number fifteen if there was a chance of speaking with Chris. She searched for her purse and thrust far too much money into the driver's hand and waved him on quickly.

Chris bowed stiffly to Mally. "I returned your reticule and bonnet."

"Thank you, Chris." She spoke lamely, conscious of Annabel standing there. "Annabel was kind enough to convey me home."

"I thank you, Annabel." He smiled at the tall girl.

"It was nothing, Chris, nothing at all. We took tea together in Petcholli's and have got to know each other quite well. I was most pleased to be of help."

He nodded. "Perhaps we should dine together again, as in old times, eh?"

Mally quivered inside. As in old times! There had been the *four* of them then!

But Annabel immediately took the straw. "Oh, I *would* like that, I would like it very much indeed."

Mally stood erect and angry. *I'll warrant you'd like it, my lady!*

Chris smiled. "Then the matter shall be arranged."

Annabel twirled her parasol. "I must take myself back to Father, he's such an ogre if I'm late—and my old grump of a chaperone will be sure to have grumped away at him, for I see that my barouche has preceded me."

Mally smiled sweetly. "Perhaps you should accompany Annabel to her door, Chris, to reassure them that she has come to no harm."

Chris's eyes went incredulously to her face and she saw the instant hurt and anger there. "But of course, I should be delighted. Come, Annabel, take my arm and we shall indeed walk the remaining yards together."

Annabel put her hand through his arm and with a tiny backward glance at Mally, she walked away with him.

Mally stood there on the pavement watching them. Why had she handled that so very, very badly? She had thrust him into Annabel's clutches, and for no good reason beyond her own stiff-necked pride. She looked around the square where the wind was bringing down the leaves with each breath now. Damn autumn! And damn all men!

Chapter 6

Mrs. Berrisford was in a fluster when Mally entered the drawing room. "Wherever have you been? I have been *frantic!* And then when Sir Christopher returned without you—"

"Don't fuss, mother. We had a small argument and I refrained from traveling a further inch with him. That is all."

"That is *all?* Sweet heavens, child, you cannot go cavorting around this *dreadful* city alone!"

"I can if I so wish, I am no maid to be chaperoned! Look, I don't wish to even talk about it, even with you, if you don't mind."

Mrs. Berrisford stared at the strained look on her daughter's face. "Lucy tells me that you and Sir Christopher are frequently at daggers drawn."

"Then Lucy had no right."

"I am your mother, Marigold, and I have every right to know these things."

"Chris and I have differences, but they are not important." Mally forced herself to smile reassuringly. *Oh, the fibs—*

"Well, Marigold, I am much chagrined that you did not see fit to confide your problems in me. After all, what's a mother for?"

Mally went to stand by the window and look out over the gardens. How could anyone confide in a mother who threatened the vapors at every turn?

Mrs. Berrisford sat down by the fire again and took up her crochet work. "I sometimes think that children were sent merely to be millstones around our necks. The very *heaviest* millstones imaginable. Your behavior this afternoon, Marigold, was worthy of a Cyprian, a demirep no less. And here was I, thinking that my elder daughter was more the *ton* than anything else in human form."

"Oh, Mother, please, shall I bring you the sal volatile? Or perhaps that curious bottle you lug around in your reticule?"

"If your father were here now he'd give you a good wigging for speaking so disrespectfully to me." Mrs. Berrisford blinked and sniffed pathetically.

"Oh, give me patience! Mother, I am just not in the mood for your mummery!"

The sniffs stopped abruptly. *"Marigold,* you have never spoken to me like this before."

"Then perhaps I should have." Mally could willingly have burst into tears. Right now the very last person on God's earth she wished to be closeted with was her mother.

The fire in the hearth shifted and sparks fluttered up the chimney like bright rubies. The clock on the escritoire chimed softly in the silent room. Mrs. Berrisford started twisting the thread on the crochet hook again, sniffing once, but no more.

After a while Mally went to sit next to her, putting her hand over hers gently. "I'm sorry, Mother—I'm a little overwrought, I fear."

Mrs. Berrisford smiled. "Yes, dear, the strain of such a

great match must surely be telling on you. I forgive you. Willingly. And now I have something to tell you. Your Mr. Paulington arrived not five minutes after you and Sir Christopher had gone."

"I did not think he would be here until later. What did he say?"

"Well, he asked me all the questions you asked me this morning. And then he asked if I had a likeness of Maria. I gave him that miniature we had done for her to give to Thomas on their marriage. He said that he would take himself to the Swan with Two Necks and make inquiries and that he would return later this evening to let us know if there is any hope."

Mally sat back. "If there's anything to be discovered, Mr. Paulington will discover it, you may be sure."

"You're probably right. I have seldom seen a man more like a ferret in my life! His looks would damn him in society, and that's a fact! But then he obviously does not care three straws for his appearance, does he?"

"No. Mother, if you will forgive me, I think I will go and lie down for a while, for my head is aching. I will join you for dinner later."

"Of course, my dear. Do you know, I really think I could close my eyes myself for a while. That journeying from Llanglyn, all the worrying about my two little chicks. Yes, a rest in that exquisite Green Room would soothe me most excellently." She wound up her crochet and pushed it back into her reticule. "Lucy tells me we are having goose for dinner tonight. I *do* love goose. And all the trimmings."

Mally smiled. "Aye, but your waistline doesn't agree with all the mounds of trimmings you seem to need!"

"Marigold," said Mrs. Berrisford archly, "*I* no longer have to trouble myself with my waistline! Only with the comfort of my interior. Until dinner then."

"Until dinner."

The goose was excellent, and Mrs. Berrisford was as good as her word, nodding appreciatively at each vegetable Digby held before her. But Mally had only a portion of goose, a roast potato, and two sprouts. Mrs. Berrisford leaned forward to examine the minute dinner on the gold-rimmed plate.

"Good gracious, child, you'll waste away!"

"I had more than enough to eat last night at Lord Dansford's ball. It will do me no harm to fast for a day or so."

"I have no intention of fasting. When do you think your Mr. Paulington will come?"

"He's not my Mr. Paulington. I don't really know. Oh, Digby, would you bring up a bottle of the Médoc with the cheese?"

"Yes, madam."

Mrs. Berrisford's eyes widened. "*Médoc* now? Good gracious, Marigold, you will have us under the table in an hour's time! We have already consumed that excellent Graves—and my capacity, being mere mortal, ends at one bottle of wine per meal, not two!"

"Mother, I feel that my capacity for wine tonight is endless, even if my capacity for food is not."

"I trust you have not become a secret tippler, Marigold."

Mally smiled. "No, Mother, whatever I do, I do in public. Besides, when you taste the Médoc, you will more than appreciate it."

"My dear, I am not a connoisseur." Mrs. Berrisford applied herself to the mountain of roast goose and trimmings.

Mally watched her. Oh, how many worlds away at this very moment were the unfortunate Mrs. Agatha Harmon? And Maria? Out of sight, out of mind? Perhaps that was unkind, for her mother had surely come on a long journey over Maria's disappearance. Maybe there was some consolation to be had in tucking into good food and deliberately forgetting the cares and woes of the world for a while.

Digby came silently into the dining room and the fluttering of the candles caught Mally's attention. "Yes, Digby, what is it?"

"Mr. Paulington has returned, madam. I have taken the liberty of showing him into the library."

Mrs. Berrisford's knife and fork clattered suddenly to her plate. "Oh, dear."

Mally glanced at the butler. "Show him in here, Digby."

"Yes, madam."

"Oh, Marigold, do you think he's found anything out?" Mrs. Berrisford mopped her mouth anxiously with her napkin.

"We are about to discover, Mother." Mally smiled, but inside she was tense and worried. Pray God he had discovered that Maria was all right—

Mr. Paulington sidled around the dining-room door and Digby shut it behind him. He stood there, a foxy-faced, foxy-eyed little man in a scruffy tweed coat which was as disreputable apparently as it had been when last Mally had seen him in this very house. And she liked him as little now as she had done then.

"Good evening, Mr. Paulington. Please come and take a seat. Would you care for a glass of wine?"

"Why thank you, thank you kindly, Mrs. St. Aubrey." He sat down on the very edge of the nearest chair, wiping the palms of his hands on his knees.

"And now, Mr. Paulington, have you any good news to impart concerning my sister?"

"Your *sister?*" He turned sharply to look at Mrs. Berrisford, who had the grace to look pink and uncomfortable. "I was under the impression as it was a friend we was looking for."

Mrs. Berrisford cleared her throat. "Well, the scandal—I thought it best not to say who she really was."

"Oh, Mother! Mr. Paulington, Maria is my younger sister. Now then, *did* you discover anything?"

"Well, it's a little confusing." He put down the miniature, surveying it for a moment and then glancing at Mally. "Reckon there *is* a likeness, now I looks at it again. But, to business, Mrs. St. Aubrey. I went to the Swan with Two Necks and made inquiries there of a fellow named Jenkins. He's the one as always meets the Hereford mails when they comes in. He said as he hadn't seen anyone as looked like the bit of muslin—beggin' your pardon—the lady in this picture. I could tell as he was not coming true with me, mind—you gets to *feel* these things—"

"*Mr.* Paulington, will you please get to the point?" Mally could have kicked his ankle in frustration.

"I had to pass a good deal of silver over his palm before he told me. Seemed as she *did* alight from the mail, and the only reason he remembers her was on account of the fact that that very evening there she was again. Going *back* again. Only this time on the Gloucester mail."

Mally stared and Mrs. Berrisford's mouth opened and closed.

He cleared his throat. "It's quite certain, Mrs. St. Aubrey. He remembers because he heard her ask if it was the Gloucester mail. Jenkins couldn't help wondering, you see, why anyone from Hereford would come all the way to London merely to get to Gloucester. Didn't seem right to him, and so he remembered her. Recognized her picture all right, an' all. Well, as luck would have it, when I was there, the Gloucester mail came in. I collared the driver and asked him about her, not thinking as he'd remember anything at all, not with all the passengers he has to account for. But he did. He remembered her when he saw the picture, because she'd not gone as far as Gloucester. Left the mail at Cirencester, he remembers, because they were an insider passenger short and she was the only woman, so they remembered her. So, if you want me to find out anything else, I'll have to take myself to Cirencester."

"Then, of course, please do that for us, Mr. Paulington, and we will more than recompense you for your troubles." She got to her feet and took a silver dish from the mantlepiece, dropping the coins inside into his outstretched hand.

He rattled the money appreciatively. "That'll more than cover my needs, Mrs. St. Aubrey. But there *is* something else you should know. I wasn't the first to be asking after her. Someone else asked, only yesterday."

"Who?"

"A country man, heavily built and rough. Ordinary-looking, from all accounts, without anything startling about him to latch on to. Wanted to know about a young lady, middle twenties, dark hair. Off of the Hereford mail. But he was a mean man, Mrs. St. Aburey, didn't offer to pay for his inquiries, so he wasn't told nothing. Slid off without another word. Mind, my suspicions was picked up, so I waited for the Hereford mail to come in—which is why I'm a little late coming here. I hoped as the driver might be the same one as brought your sister up to London."

"And was it?"

"No. But he knew something, for all that. He was at the inn in Hereford a few days back when a man who fitted the description of this country feller came in and started asking about a young lady. The booking chap there said as she'd bought for London. Whereupon the country gent did exactly the same. Someone, Mrs. St. Aubrey, is as anxious as you to find your sister."

Mrs. Berrisford squeaked, her eyes wide. "Oh, dear,

this sounds so very mysterious and frightening. Whatever can it all be about, Marigold?"

Mally saw the worry and alarm growing in her mother's eyes. "Oh, it is surely merely a coincidence, Mother. Is that not so, Mr. Paulington?" She flashed him a warning glance.

"Oh, yes. Yes, indeed, I just thought I would mention it." Mr. Paulington's chair scraped loudly as he stood. "Don't let it worry you, Mrs. Berrisford. Well, I'll be off then, and I'll do my best, you may be sure. Good evening to you, ladies."

"Good evening, Mr. Paulington. And thank you." Mally inclined her head.

A short while after he had gone, Digby came in with the bottle of wine, followed by a wide-eyed, nervous maid carrying the cheese board.

The butler cleared his throat as he set the bottle on the table. "Madam, I do not wish to alarm you at all, but I am concerned that someone may be watching the house. From out there by the trees in the square."

Chapter 7

Mrs. Berrisford looked fit to faint. "Oh, we are to be murdered in our beds, just as poor dear Agatha was!"

"Mother! Don't be silly! It's probably a burglar wondering if it would be worth breaking in here. Will you show me, Digby?" Mally tried desperately to conceal her own instant fear.

"Yes, madam, if you will follow me. It was Lucy who first noticed him, a few moments ago when she was drawing the curtains of your dressing room. He was smoking, you see, and she saw the glow of his cigar."

Mrs. Berrisford hesitated as she saw everyone leaving the room, and then abruptly she got to her feet and hurried after them.

Digby extinguished the oil lamps on the landing and they approached the tall window overlooking the square. They pressed close to the window, except for the frightened little maid who hovered behind them anxiously.

Digby pointed through the lace curtain. "There, madam. By the third tree from your right. Yes. Do you see him? He's only a shadow—but *there!* He's lit another cigar!"

Mally gently pulled the lace curtain aside to see more clearly. The square was misty and cold, and the occasional leaf drifted to the wet grass. A carriage moved along the far side of the green. It was Chris's and she remembered that he was dining with the Earl of Hartmore, Annabel's father. The cobbles gleamed damply and the man's silhouette was just visible in the gray haze.

They were so intent upon watching that they did not hear Lucy coming down from the floor above, nor did they hear her exclamation of annoyance at finding the main landing in darkness. She hurried back upstairs and lifted an oil lamp from its holder, and then came down again. The light flooded onto the landing behind the window, picking out Mally quite clearly as she peered around the heavy lace curtain.

"Lucy!" Mrs. Berrisford squealed in dismay, gesturing the old nurse away. "He'll see us all now!"

But it was too late, for the man had seen Mally's outline. He stamped out the cigar and melted back among the trees. There were no fleeing footsteps to hear this time, but the coldness she had experienced before slithered back over Mally as she stood there. Digby took Mrs. Berrisford's arm, for she seemed about to faint clean away, and he supported her back into the warm dining room.

Mally remained by the window for a while. Chris's carriage had passed from sight beyond St. Blaise's now and across the square the Earl's house was a blaze of color and lights. But down in the square, the trees were dark and mysterious, a cobweb of inky shadows and strange shapes. She turned away and took a long breath; she must hide her unease from her mother.

In the dining room Mrs. Berrisford was accepting a glass of wine from the patient Digby, and the little maid was still wavering around by the door, seeming to be on the point of dissolving into tears at any moment. Lucy stood by the table looking upset, and Mally went to her.

"Don't fret now, Lucy, it wasn't your fault. I'll tell you what, you and Digby go to the kitchens, and take this poor maid with you, and have some of the best brandy to set you all up again."

When she was alone with her mother again, she poured herself a very large glass of the Médoc.

Mrs. Berrisford watched her. "I begin to find your consumption of wine rather alarming, Marigold."

"If you think *I* drink heavily, then I pray you are never invited to a society dinner party, for then the capacity of some ladies of repute would absolutely stagger you. Now, let me sit down and get my breath back. I—I wonder what he was watching us for? He must have been a hopeful burglar, don't you think?"

"Or something more sinister."

"Oh, Mother, don't say such things, please."

"We would not even have known he was there had it not been for Lucy. I shall be locking my door again tonight, and you must do the same, Marigold."

"Let's change the subject, shall we? I met the new owner of Castell Melyn today."

"That *man!*"

"Why ever do you feel like that about Mr. Vallender? I found him most charming."

"He is odious in the extreme."

"Oh. Well, we will have to beg to differ on that point for the time being—until he proves to *me* that he is odious."

"I know nothing good about him. Nothing at all. As I have already said. He is a harborer of murderers and seducers of young women!"

"Goodness, and here's my good self with an invitation to visit him there."

"You wouldn't, Marigold!"

"Why ever not? I found him most agreeable. Did you realize that he is an old friend of both Chris and Daniel?"

Mrs. Berrisford stared at her. "Not *that* Dickon Vallender? The boy they went to school with?"

"Yes. That's why he bought the castle, because he knew Llanglyn was where Daniel came from. He didn't know Daniel was dead or that he had been married."

"Would that he had forgotten where Daniel came from then."

"I found him pleasant."

"So you keep saying, Marigold. Are you sure that you and Sir Christopher quarreled about an ordinary difference? Was it perhaps your delight in this Mr. Vallender?"

"No, Mother, it was not about Mr. Vallender."

"Then why has not Sir Christopher called here tonight? I recognized his carriage a moment ago."

Mally looked at her glass. "He is dining with the Earl of Hartmore."

"Quite a party they must be making of it, judging by the lights and so on over there." Mrs. Berrisford looked carefully at her. "Was it not the Earl's daughter Sir Christopher was once expected to marry?"

"Lady Annabel Murchison. Yes, Mother."

"A tall piece? Golden hair?"

"Yes."

"Mm."

Mally looked sharply at her. "Why do you mutter like that?"

"Because while you were surveying the man in the square, I happened to glance across at the Earl's house. I could see straight into the drawing room before the curtains were drawn."

"And?"

"And I saw Sir Christopher and Lady Annabel sitting very cosily together. Very cosily."

Daniel! Daniel St. Aubrey! You let me out of here this instant! Do you hear me! The cold, cold darkness was all around her, velvety and close, pressing in on her all over again. *Daniel, please, I'm frightened.* The icy air seemed to move over her like a ghostly breath.

And Daniel's voice. So far away. *Come and find me, Mally. Come and find me.*

Daniel! The sepulchral air breathed again.

Abruptly the nightmare was gone. Mally lay there shaking in the warm bed. The nightmare had gone, but its threads still lingered in the room, threads like cobwebs to cling to her across the years. She stared at the tiny night light, its steady little glow visible through the velvet drapes of the bed. The sheets smelled of lavender. And they were warm. Not cold and damp like a grave—

The quiet of the night was absolute. Except— She turned her head slightly at a faint, stealthy sound. At the door. She froze with a sudden new fear as the night light quivered a little in its dish as a cool draft spread through the room from the opened door. The velvet curtains of the bed moved slightly as a hand drew them aside.

The terror rose to a crescendo and she began to scream. The hand vanished and heavy steps retreated toward the door. Still screaming she dragged the bedclothes away and pushed past the still trembling curtains. The door of the room was wide open, and as she ran out onto the landing and leaned over the banisters, a figure stood down in the hallway, the hood of its cloak pulled over its face although it was staring up at her, motionless.

She screamed again and the figure's frozen immobility vanished. With one or two steps it was by the front door which had already been unbolted. The doors swung heavily, letting in the mist and cold of the night, and then the intruder was gone. Mally thought she could hear footsteps out in the night. And then nothing.

"Miss Mall? Miss Mall, whatever is it?"

She turned to see Lucy's frightened face lit by the single candle she was holding. Her gray hair was in one long plait hanging down over her right shoulder, and one hand was clutching the drawstring at the throat of her nightgown.

"Oh, Lucy—" Mally clung weakly to the banisters. "Someone tried to get into my room, he was at the very bed itself! Oh, if I hadn't woken up—!"

"Marigold?" Mrs. Berrisford's key rattled and she peeped cautiously out of the room. "Marigold? Was that you screaming, or was I dreaming?" Her face, bereft of rouge, looked podgy and pale, and her mousy hair was revealed without its usual wig cover.

Lucy put her arm gently around Mally's shaking shoulders. "Come on down to the library, Miss Mall, the fire will still be in there. You've had a dreadful shock."

Mally looked down into the empty hall again, looking through the shimmering crystals of the chandelier. Surely she had not imagined it—

But then Digby came up from the basements, his old nightcap pulled over his balding head and his dressing gown tied firmly around his bony body. He went to the doors and closed them, pausing before finally closing the second one to look across the square.

"What is it, Digby?"

"Sir Christopher is just leaving the Earl's house, madam."

Chris. "Go and bring him, Digby, I beg of you."

"Marigold!" Mrs. Berrisford emerged a little more from the haven of her room. "You cannot!"

"I want him here, Mother!" She looked over at Digby. "If you please."

The butler straightened his nightcap self-consciously, rearranged his dressing gown, and stepped out down the steps into the night.

Lucy steered Mally down the stairs to the floor below

and into the leather-filled warmth of the library. The fire glowed softly behind its guard and the spines of the books ranged around on their shelves looked soothing and comforting as Mally sat in Daniel's favorite chair by the fire.

They heard light steps coming up from the hallway and then Chris was there, tossing his top hat onto the table.

"Mally?" His eyes were anxious and he brought the scent of cigar smoke with him, clinging to his velvet coat.

"Oh, Chris—" She stood and ran to him.

He caught her close, his fingers twining in her thick dark hair, and his lips were soft as he kissed her. "It's all right now, sweetheart, I'm here."

"Don't leave me tonight, Chris, please." She pressed against him, her face buried in the frill and lace of his shirt.

"I won't. I promise."

Chapter 8

Chris put down the *Morning Chronicle* as Mally entered the dining room the following morning. He stood and held his hands out to her. "Do you feel a little better this morning?"

She pulled a wry face. "I feel a little foolish this morning, that is for sure."

"Foolish? But you had every right to be frightened." He pulled her into his arms. "I have set Digby to check through the entire house and gardens to see if anything has been stolen, but on a cursory glance myself I could see nothing."

"My noisy awakening probably finished the burglary before it had properly begun." *If it was a burglary—* The thought slipped through her mind quite unexpectedly.

There was a discreet knock at the door and Digby came in. "Good morning, madam."

"Good morning, Digby." She stepped self-consciously away from Chris.

"Sir Christopher," said the butler, "I have done as you bade me, commencing with the gardens. And it seems most probable that the fellow entered from the back lane between this house and Lady Simmonds's, for the ivy has been torn from the wall by the dovecote. The kitchen door has been forced and I have sent for a locksmith to replace the damaged lock. But on going through the house itself, sir, I could find nothing. Nothing at all. I would say that not one single thing has been touched or even moved. I even set the house maids and parlor maids to check, and they swear that everything looks as it should."

Chris nodded. "Thank you, Digby. Will you send someone to report the matter to the necessary authorities, although I know they can do nothing."

"Yes, Sir Christopher." The butler left the dining room again.

Chris pulled a chair out at the table for her. "Well, you must be right, Mally. He chose your room to begin on—and that proved his undoing, eh?" He smiled at her.

She settled herself, and took his hand quickly before he went to sit.

"Chris, forgive my sending for you so dramatically and publicly like that. It was not at all the thing, was it?"

"Under the circumstances, sweetheart, you were quite justified—and I would be hurt to think you would hesitate merely on the grounds of what *looks* correct. Besides, I seized the chance of flying to your side with a good deal of alacrity, I promise you." He raised her hand to his lips. "Think no more of it."

"Do you think the authorities will find anything?"

"No. If nothing was stolen then there will be nothing to turn up to offer a clue. Whoever it was came and went empty-handed. End of chapter, I fear."

End of chapter. Was it? Again the unbidden thought slid into her head. It had been no burglary, for the intruder had come directly to the bed. To *her* bed— As she took some crisp bacon from the silver dish on the table, she pondered the man in the square the night before. He had been little more than a silhouette. A silhouette in a box coat. Like some country man back in Breconshire and hardly like a Londoner— She stared at the bacon. That was it. He had looked like a country man. And a country man had been at the Swan with Two Necks asking about Maria.

"Mally? I'd warrant a penny now would purchase some intriguing thoughts."

"Mm?"

"Your thoughts." Chris stirred his coffee, watching her.

"Oh, I was just wondering what the fellow came here for, that's all." She sounded open and honest, she decided, even if she knew inside that she wasn't being either. She wanted to tell him about Maria, but then she had promised her mother that Maria's reputation would come before all.

"Don't let it worry you anymore, sweetheart. He's gone and that's the end of it. Now, let us change to a more pleasing topic. I have arranged a dinner party for a week tomorrow. A party for four."

"Four? You and myself, presumably, but who are the other two to be?"

"Richard Vallender. And—Annabel."

"Oh. My, she *was* busy last evening, wasn't she?"

He smiled. "How sweet to see the stirrings of jealousy in *you* for a change, jealousy as ill-founded as my own. Before I left for Hartmore's yesterday, Richard called. He was on his way to Benleigh Square and realized how close he was passing to me. I took the opportunity of nailing him to a set time and place for dinner with us. Annabel then seemed the obvious choice for a fourth."

"Obvious indeed." Mally raised an eyebrow. "I trust you enjoyed yourself yesterday. From all the lights and so on one would have imagined at the very least a coming-out ball was in progress. You told me it was a dinner with her father."

"And so it was. I *did* notice the lights myself, though." He grinned. "I don't get a welcome like that when I come here."

"Damn her."

"I'm flattered."

"And damn you too."

"How kind." He sat back then. "Tell me, you have friends in Benleigh Square, don't you? Sarah Chitterly?"

"Yes. Sarah and her aunt live there. Number seven."

"I thought so."

She watched him curiously. "Why do you ask?"

"Richard had paid off his chaise, knowing that he was so close to his destination. He asked me which way around to go to get to number three. I may be mistaken, but is that not the address of that German doctor who's creating such a name for himself at the moment? Schiller? Schriller? Stiller? It begins with 'S' anyway."

"Yes. Sarah lives four houses away from him. I had tea with her one afternoon and we amused ourselves by counting the carriages calling there."

Chris poured himself another coffee. "I don't somehow think Richard was calling socially. He seemed a little tense. Oh, nothing that anyone who didn't know him well would notice, but then I knew him very well once and things like that remain with you."

"I hope you are wrong. Oh, you must be, for he looked in rude health to me the other day. Yesterday. Oh, was it really only yesterday? It seems more like last week. So much has happened." Mally looked away. Yes, a lot had happened.

"You're right, he did look healthy. Oh, well, perhaps it *was* social. Tell me, how is your sister? I notice that she did not come with your mother."

She dropped her fork. "Maria?"

"How many sisters have you?"

"Oh, she is well enough. Visiting relatives, I believe."

Oh, how she hated lying to him, but somehow— He was Richard Vallender's friend; and it could be that Richard might know something about Maria. What, Mally couldn't imagine, but she just knew she wished to say nothing to Chris, both because she had promised her mother, and because she felt that it was the wisest thing to do for the moment.

She stared across the room at the bobbing Michaelmas daisies in the garden. The man in the square— If he *had* been the same man who asked about Maria at the inn, what would he be watching this house for? Why, for Maria, of course. It was obvious. And what would he perhaps have thought when he saw a woman like Maria outlined in that window when Lucy had brought the lamp? He would think she was Maria, for at that distance there would be no telling the difference as there was a great likeness between the two Berrisford sisters. The daisies swayed as the breeze brought a shower of red and gold leaves down from the beech tree. There was a connection between Maria and Castell Melyn, and Mally decided there and then that she would foster any burgeoning friendship with Mr. Richard Vallender.

Chris cleared his throat. "I believe, Mally, that we are about to be joined by your good lady mother. Listen."

They listened to the loud voice from the landing above. "Lucy? Lucy, where have you put it? I wish to know immediately. What? In where? Good heavens, you goose, it will be creased beyond redemption!"

Mally groaned. "Do you know, Chris, if it had not been for Lucy all these years, I think both Maria and myself would have been long since incarcerated in Bedlam!"

"How long is she staying here?"

"I don't know."

"Perhaps we should introduce her to old Hartmore. That would be a grand thing, eh? They could put an end to each other, he by boring her, and she by driving him to distraction!"

Mally laughed. "I don't think even Mother deserves the Earl."

"Maybe not. *Nobody* deserves him. How he managed to sire a beauty like Annabel I'll never know. I often wonder if her late mother knew something she never divulged to anyone."

"Most likely. The Earl has brown eyes and so did Annabel's mother. And so has every other Hartmore I can think of. And yet Annabel has green eyes. One does wonder, doesn't one?"

"Scandalmonger."

Chapter 9

"There, Lucy, what do you think?" Mally twirled before the nurse.

"Miss Mall, you'll finish her completely."

"I hope so." Mally smoothed the folds of blue mantua silk and the soft material shimmered in the firelight. But it was not triumphing over Annabel which was uppermost in her mind about tonight's dinner party, it was meeting Richard Vallender again. Since her breakfast with Chris after the "burglary" she had become more and more convinced in her own mind that it had had something to do with Maria. Tonight she might be able to find out more about her sister's friendship with the late Mr. York.

Lucy smiled fondly. Blue was Mally's best color, and tonight she looked exquisite with her dark curls piled so expertly by the ruby pin so that they cascaded in ringlets at the back of her head. And the Italian silk clung to her body when she moved, outlining the curves to perfection. Then Lucy looked at Mally's face. "But a little more rouge would make you look healthier."

"It would make me look feverish."

"Better than liverish. Besides, it's *in* at the moment to wear rouge, even I know that."

"I know—but I've more than enough natural color."

"Maybe you do—normally. But you've had late nights in plenty and a few upsets, and you're worrying about your sister. To say nothing of whether you are doing the right thing in marrying Sir Christopher. You look *pale!* Come on now, just let me brush a little Spanish wool on your cheeks.

Mally gave in and allowed Lucy to color her cheeks. "Have you hung the chenille lace shawl?"

"Of course, I don't forget things like that. Be sure to wear it properly now, sweeting, for it's warmer than your others and silk is *not* the most sensible of materials for this time of year."

"I'm wearing this gown because I know Chris likes me in it, and because Annabel knows he does too! Oh, God, she said she'd keep me on my toes and she was right. I only wish she were less beautiful and dazzling!"

"Well, she's got the height to carry everything off, has that one. And her hair is the brightest *natural* gold I've seen in years." Lucy nodded approvingly. "And she knows well to wear different greens all the time. It's her device."

"Don't deflate me, Lucy, I beg of you." Mally looked at her reflection again. "Perhaps I should have worn the white gauze—"

"That pale blue is perfectly good, Miss Mall. Now then, I've put your white gloves and reticule on the dressing table. Shall you wear a necklace?"

"I don't know. No—" Mally smiled and took off her engagement ring. "I shall wear no jewels at all, except my ring over my glove. *That* will be something to rub Lady Annabel's nose in the mud with!"

"Sweeting, I don't think you need to rub her nose in any more than you already have done."

"And I shall change the ruby pin for that green enameled butterfly Maria's betrothed bought for me in Italy—it will catch the green in the ring. There. Now I feel I can take on the world and his wife—and any predatory titled lady!"

She was pulling on the slender white kid gloves when Digby knocked upon the door. "Yes, Digby, what is it?"

"Mr. Paulington is here, Madam. I have shown him secretly into the library and Mrs. Berrisford does not know he is here, as you directed."

Mally took a long breath. "Yes, thank you, Digby, I shall be in the library directly."

The butler closed the door again and Mally bit her lip. Lucy patted her shoulder. "Don't let anything spoil your evening now, for dining out with Sir Christopher and his friend will do you good."

"That is easier said than done, isn't it, Lucy? What if he's discovered something dreadful?"

"Good evening, Mr. Paulington. Have you discovered anything?"

He scrambled to his feet hurriedly, for he had been lazing very comfortably in Daniel's chair. "Oh, good evening, Mrs. St. Aubrey."

"Please sit down again, Mr. Paulington."

"Thank you. Thank you kindly. Well, Mrs. St. Aubrey, I have managed to discover something concerning your sister. She did indeed leave the mail at Cirencester and spent that night in a hostelry named the Castle. On the following morning she was called for by a gentleman driving a phaeton."

"She was *called* for?"

"Yes, madam. And she was expecting him, whoever he was. I got a description of some sort from the innkeeper, but unfortunately the fellow was more interested in the phaeton than in the driver. Now then, yes, here it is. He was quite tall, lean, with dark hair—he thinks—reasonably well togged out but no Corinthian or beau. As I said, the innkeeper was more interested in the phaeton. Seems it belonged to one of his rivals, a posting house in Gloucester by the name of the Rose and Crown."

"A post *phaeton*? That is surely something new!"

"Seems this Kennett of the Rose and Crown has done well with the phaeton, there's many folk fancy themselves up on a high-flyer like that. It is a dark brown drag, well lacquered and polished, and it has red wheels, with a yellow crown device thing in the center of each lamp—the crown of the Rose and Crown. The rose is painted on the back and gets covered with mud with each puddle! Anyway, that was what I discovered. So, I took myself on the next stage to Gloucester and looked up this Mr. Kennett at the Rose and Crown. The phaeton was hired to go to Cirencester and then to Hereford. Kennett sent a boy to Hereford to pick it up two days later, as agreed. He was pleased with himself too, for some rector or other wanted to come to Gloucester and paid for the use of the phaeton, so I reckon that drag's more than paid for itself three times over. So, Mrs. St. Aubrey, the trail led me back right to where it started. Hereford."

"Did you go there too? To wherever the phaeton was left?"

"Yes, but there wasn't much time to make inquiries, for the mail was about to leave and I didn't want to have to hang around another day. The gentleman left the phaeton at the inn during the night. No one can remember it arriving—there was something of a junketing there that night, for the innkeeper had married again. Anyway it was there come the morning. No one saw the gentleman or the young lady. So that's it, I'm afraid, the trail has run out. I tried, I offered various sums to various people, but they just did not know."

"And no one could give a better description of the

gentleman other than that he was tall, dark, and not particularly fashionable?"

"No, madam. When he hired the phaeton at Gloucester it was a wet day and the man wore his hat well down and a cloak which flapped around him like a live thing. Hid anything of notice about him fairly sure." Mr. Paulington got to his feet. "To my mind, Mrs. St. Aubrey, it seems certain that your sister knew this man before she left Llanglyn and that the full intention was to run off with him. The fiddling around at London and so on was just to throw off any trail—they were not to know that *I* would be following them." He sniffed proudly.

"They still succeeded in the end, didn't they?"

"Eh? Well, yes, I suppose I must admit that. Though I *could* go back and try—" Then he shook his head. "No, it'd be more than any needle in any haystack you care to mention. There's roads in and out of Hereford like nobody's business, and the night's long this time of year, they could have gone *any*where. I have to admit defeat, Mrs. St. Aubrey, much as it grieves me to say so."

Mally opened her reticule, where she had earlier placed a sum with which to pay him. "Thank you, Mr. Paulington."

"I only wish—"

"Not to worry, no doubt in her own good time my sister will return to us. Thank you again, Mr. Paulington."

"Thank *you*, Mrs. St. Aubrey."

She heard the front doors close after him, and then she left the library and went into the drawing room.

"Oh, there you are, Mother. How do I look?" She smiled brightly, much more brightly than she felt.

Mrs. Berrisford put down the eternal crochet work. "Oh, most perfect, Marigold, *most* perfect. Sir Christopher will surely fall in love with you all over again."

Mally went to the table where Digby had earlier placed a decanter of Malmsey. She poured two glasses of it, more to give herself a moment to consider than because she wanted a drink. What should she tell her mother? Maria had eloped, and had given not one thought to the misery she caused her mother. And it would appear that the man came from somewhere reasonably close to Llanglyn, for why else would the trail end in Hereford? Perhaps he was already known to her mother— Anything was possible. But who was the other man searching for Maria? The decanter rattled against the glasses, for her hand was shaking. Well, whatever it was all about, for the moment the main thing was to reassure her mother.

"Mother, I have just been speaking with Mr. Paulington."

"Oh, dear. It's not going to be bad news, is it? Oh, it is, I can see it in your eyes, you've something *dreadful* to impart!" The crochet slipped to the floor as Mrs. Berrisford's hands flew to her mouth.

"No, no, Mother, don't immediately think the worst like that. Listen now." Mally crouched beside her mother's chair and put the glasses on the floor. "I think we have to accept that Maria has eloped. She was met by a gentleman at Cirencester and drove off in his phaeton with him." Best let the trail end at Cirencester—

"A *gentle*man?"

"Yes. Not a leviathan of the *haut ton*, I fancy, but nonetheless a gentleman."

Mrs. Berrisford searched her face with hurt expression. "But why could she not have left word? Or sent word? Why leave me to worry so, especially when she knew I was already upset about poor, dear Agatha. I did not think she could be so cruel to her own mother."

"Oh, you know Maria. She just probably did not think—and she was upset herself, about Mr. York. After all he was her friend, you said so yourself."

"Yes, indeed I did. Mind you, I was convinced it was more than a mere friendship she had with him, *convinced*.

It seems I was wrong. Oh, dear, I don't know what to think anymore. You are *sure* she has eloped?"

"What else can it be? She was met at the inn in Cirencester by a gentleman and went off with him. No one was forcing her."

"Oh, the disgrace. What am I to say to the Clevelys? I shall never be able to hold my head up again in Llanglyn, never!"

"Of course you will."

"But Marigold, who was the other man asking about Maria then?" Mrs. Berrisford sat up suddenly as the thought struck her.

"We don't know that he *was* asking for Maria, do we? He could have been looking for anyone. Now then, have a little sip of this, it will do you good." Mally hurriedly picked up the glass, anxious to gloss over the uncomfortable thought of the country man.

Mrs. Berrisford sipped the wine. "I suppose I shall have to draw myself up for the fray."

"I beg your pardon?"

"I shall have to go back to Llanglyn and prepare for whatever. Oh dear, it's a daunting prospect. What shall I say? When they inquire after Maria, whatever am I to say? I let them all believe she had come to stay with you, d'you see. I cannot *bear* chitter-chatter."

"Then say that Maria is with me."

"But Marigold, I was hoping—counting upon—"

"Yes?"

"I would like you to return to Llanglyn with me. Just for a little while. It *would* be a comfort."

"Then we shall just have to brave it out together and say that we do not know where Maria is, shan't we? I mean, it cannot be kept a secret for long anyway, and the Clevelys' noses are always to the ground—they won't miss a thing."

Mrs. Berrisford drained her glass in one gulp. "Mercy above, I feel quite faint."

"Well, when Chris asked about Maria I just said that she was visiting relatives."

"And what did he say to that?"

"Nothing, he just accepted it. Oh, I suppose we could always invent a distant aunt or something."

"*Very* distant. On your father's side." Mrs. Berrisford took Mally's untouched glass from its place on the floor. "Yes, yes, I think that is an admirable solution."

"Mother, it's only putting off the inevitable, you know."

"Yes, Marigold, but maybe we'll hear from Maria in the meantime. I will not give up hope. You *will* return with me for a while, though, won't you?"

"Yes, of course I will."

"Good. At the end of this week then."

"Good heavens—so quickly?"

"Yes, my mind is made up. I cannot bear anticipating anything unpleasant, so the sooner I return the better I will feel. Besides, I do not much care for London."

Mally smiled. "All right, I will make arrangements for us to travel at the end of the week. But, Mother, I will have to tell Chris the truth, for it is not right to conceal such things from him."

Mrs. Berrisford nodded unhappily. "I suppose so. Oh, dear, I wish your dear father was with me now. How I curse that brute of a horse that killed him so cruelly."

"Father should not have taken that hedge in the first place; it was not the horse's fault."

"Shame on you, Marigold." But Mrs. Berrisford smiled. "Dear James, he was so *dashing*. And so courageous."

And so pig-headed about hunting. But Mally refrained from further comment. "Listen—I think that is the carriage Chris is sending for me. Are you sure you'll be all right?"

"Yes, yes, my dear, you go along now. I think I shall take myself to my bed in a little while—all this worry has left me quite drained. Quite drained." Mrs. Berrisford looked up at her daughter. "You know, you really do look your best in that shade of blue. Daniel always said so."

"I wear it tonight because Chris likes it, Mother."

"Then you may for once please both your inner self and Sir Christopher, may you not?"

Mally looked down at her in surprise, for it was hardly ever that such perception came from her mother—

A few minutes later, with her shawl wrapped around her against the chill of the night, she climbed into the carriage which was to take her to her second meeting with Richard Vallender. *And let it please prove useful. In some way or other.*

Chapter 10

After dinner the four retired to the splendid drawing room of the house in Pendleton Square, with Mally hoping the after-dinner conversation would prove fruitful. The perfume of sandalwood hung in the warm air from the potpourri jars set by the fire, and it was a perfume which went well with the Eastern furnishings of the room. The alcoves by the marble fireplace were filled with tall dark cupboards covered with wonderful carvings of weird creatures and plants and strange shapes which defied description. On either side of the windows stood ebony elephants with sharp tusks which threatened to tear the clothes of anyone unwary enough to pass too close, and the curtains hanging at the windows were woven with unusual birds and flowers. The tables were low, of beaten or carved brass, and seemed as if waiting for cushions to be set beside them— The chairs and sofas themselves were woven with Indian patterns, gold threads glinting among the bright reds and blues.

But it was the new addition to the room which immediately caught Mally's eye. It was a black statue of a goddess—or was it a god—her hollow eyes staring horribly across the room, as if seeing all. Her hands were clasped before her as if in prayer, but the fingers were long and crooked, for all the world like hooks or claws, and her body was misshapen and grotesque. She stood beneath a cloth-of-gold canopy, and Mally did not like the atmosphere she created.

"Oh, Chris, what is that horrible thing?"

"That, Mally, is the goddess Deyna. She Who Sees All."

"Well named, somehow," remarked Richard, lounging back on a sofa. His dark purple coat looked almost black in the dim light cast by the candles. "Ye gods, Chris, when are the turban-headed acrobats to come in? I remember your partiality for things Eastern, but this somehow comes as a surprise."

Annabel looked at the goddess again. "Where did you get her? I haven't seen her before."

Mally glanced at her. Was that a subtle reminder that she, Annabel Murchison, had once been a frequent visitor to this house? For once Annabel had chosen not to wear green. She was a picture in rose pink, her golden hair worn *à la Madonna* with a center parting and flowing loose curls on the crown of her head. A diamond necklace winked and flashed at her throat, drawing attention to the daring *décolletage* of the satin gown, although such an additional piece of eye-catching was hardly necessary with so brief a garment, thought Mally uncharitably. She felt almost prudish in the blue Italian silk.

Chris looked at the statue. "It came yesterday, a gift from my brother Henry. He had it shipped from India."

Annabel shuddered. "Remind me to kick his ankle the next time I dance with him. Why such a revolting object for this beautiful room? Just as revolting as that dreadful snake basket you keep over there. Each time I see it I am convinced that it is still occupied."

Chris smiled, bowing over her hand, his slender body made more slender by the black velvet he wore. "I assure you, dearest Annabel, that the basket is quite, quite empty."

"*Gott sei Dank,*" murmured Richard. "Mrs. St. Aubrey, in view of the strange and somewhat disturbing tastes of your prospective husband, perhaps you would like to reconsider the marriage, for the Lord knows what *else* his tastes run to."

She smiled. "Ah, but I am perhaps attracted by such anticipation, Mr. Vallender."

"You shock me, madam." He pretended astonishment.

"I doubt that, Mr. Vallender." She looked at him again. Was it possible that he knew something about Maria?

But Chris was speaking of the statue again. "Of course, Annabel, you realize *why* you feel so uncomfortable before the goddess? It is because she sees all and knows all." He glanced at Richard and winked.

"So does my chaperone," laughed Annabel, but she did look at the goddess's hollow eyes uncomfortably once more.

Chris took her hand again. "Come and stand before her, if you dare reveal your innermost self to her."

Mally looked suspiciously at him. "Chris, is this a trick?"

His eyes were innocent. "Trick? Me?"

"Yes. You." She turned toward Richard quickly as she heard his smothered laugh.

Annabel heard it too. "Oh, so you think I shall be tricked, do you? Very well, Chris, show me the wonders of this horrible thing in the corner."

"Annabel—" Mally put out her hand, but Richard caught it and pulled it back, his eyes shining.

"Let us see," he whispered.

Annabel glanced back. "Come on, you two, it's not fair that I should be the only one."

Richard stood, holding his hand out to Mally. "Come, *I* will protect you from She Who Sees All."

"I am not reassured by that somehow."

"Now I am devastated. How could you be so cruel to me?"

"Instinct."

He smiled, leading her purposefully toward the corner where Chris and Annabel stood waiting.

It was dark, their shadows falling over the black statue, and close to Deyna seemed more menacing and unearthly. And Chris's voice matched the atmosphere, being low and hypnotic.

"Deyna, She Who Sees All, goddess of life and death, guardian of the entrance to paradise or the gateway into perdition. When you stand before her you are judged, for her eye will fall upon you." He drew Annabel even closer. "There," he whispered, "look into her eyes and let her see the truth—"

Mally's hand tightened in Richard's as she watched Annabel lean toward the statue. She was so intent upon Annabel and Chris that she did not notice Richard's arm around her waist in the darkness of the corner, and neither did she notice Chris touch something at the base of the statue with his foot.

As Annabel looked deep into Deyna's hollow eyes they suddenly shone with vivid green light. She squealed and leaped back, while Chris began to laugh. Mally shrank against Richard instinctively as the horrible glowing eyes seemed to grow in the darkness.

Annabel glared at Chris. "You beast!"

"Oh, I could not resist it, for you were so perfect!"

"You are still a beast!"

Richard took his arm away from Mally's waist. "Would that my good friend had many more such diversions, for I thoroughly enjoy comforting you."

She smiled. "I had not even noticed, Mr. Vallender."

"Ah, me, demolished again."

Chris put his arm lightly around Annabel's shoulder. "Forgive me, Annabel. I did not mean to frighten you, but I just could not resist it."

"If I have a single gray hair in the morning, I shall sue you."

"Come, take a glass of liqueur with me and forgive my gross behavior."

Annabel glanced at Mally, obviously affected by Chris's closeness. She moved away a little, and Mally saw how much that small step cost her. "Tell me, Chris," said Annabel, "how did you do it? I mean, how were the eyes made to light up like that?"

"It's an old trick, the priests used it in Deyna's temple. There is a candle burning inside her, and if you touch this knob down here then a shield drops away from the eyes, letting the candlelight shine through the green glass eyes." He smiled again. "Henry put in precise instructions, as related to him by a former priest. I gather Deyna is discredited now—she didn't see enough!"

Richard laughed. "Maybe *she* didn't, but I fancy Lady Annabel has tonight!"

Annabel nodded with feeling. "How right you are, Mr. Vallender, but I shall have my revenge, of that you may be sure."

Richard rolled his eyes. "Chris, I envy you!"

They sat down again, and somehow now the presence of Deyna was no longer oppressive. Annabel settled herself carefully, arranging the gathers of satin to their best advantage.

"Tell me, Mr. Vallender," she said, "what decided you to return to England after all this time?"

"There was little to keep me there."

"All those years and you can say that?"

"Yes. My wife died in childbed, the baby died too, the plantation was not longer paying its way due to a blight which I could not rid it of, and I had a desire to kick my heels free of America for a while."

"And so you just sold up and came back?"

"Yes. I saw the advertisement for Castell Melyn and remembered that Llanglyn was where Daniel hailed from. It seemed the perfect solution."

She searched his face. "And was it?"

"The perfect solution? I have yet to discover. It is interesting, though, for it has a ghost."

"Ghost?" Annabel's eyes shone suddenly. "Oh, do tell me you have seen it, Mr. Vallender, for I have yet to meet anyone who has *really* seen a ghost."

"Unfortunately she is rather shy. I am informed by the local doctor, Dr. Towers, that she is the ghost of a certain Lady Jacquetta de Winter, a medieval noblewoman whose husband walled her up for being unfaithful to him.

Mally shuddered. "Don't."

"You are from Llanglyn, Mrs. St. Aubrey, and so you must know the story."

"Yes."

Annabel was curious at Mally's reaction. "What's wrong, Mally?"

"Nothing."

Richard searched her face. "Surely you do not believe the tale, Mrs. St. Aubrey?"

"No. It's just that I was shut away in part of your castle once a long time ago and I have never been more terrified in my life. I dream about it even now."

Annabel's eyes shone excitedly. "It sounds truly skin-crawling! Doesn't it, Chris?"

He laughed. "Not particularly, but then I obviously do not have your vivid imagination! And I am surprised at you, Annabel, after that exhibition before poor Deyna a few minutes ago!"

"But, Chris, I've always wanted to go to a real haunted house. I've been to several which *call* themselves haunted, but they've each been a dreadful disappointment. This one sounds so—so *genuine!*"

"Because you want it to be, Annabel." Chris grinned at her. "Well, then, put it to the test. Prevail upon Richard here to invite you to his eerie—or should that be eyrie?—establishment on his Breconshire mountain. More than that, prevail upon him to invite us all so that we may all shiver and tremble."

Annabel turned to Richard immediately. "Oh, could we? I should *love* it, truly I should!"

Richard's eyes flickered momentarily to Mally. It was such a brief glance that she thought perhaps she had imagined it, and there was a slight hesitation before he smiled at Annabel. "I do not know that my poor castle is grand enough for an earl's daughter, Lady Annabel."

"What nonsense," said Annabel. "You are backing out, aren't you? You have been fibbing about that ghost!"

"No, I have not been fibbing. And if I had been, then you must accuse Mrs. St. Aubrey of aiding and abetting me."

"Then let us come and prove for ourselves."

Richard smiled at Annabel's glittering eyes. "I had not imagined you to be such a dedicated ghost-hunter, my lady."

"I am—but they always evaporate whenever I am near! Oh, *please*, Mr. Vallender."

Mally caught Richard's swift glance yet again, and sensed immediately that any reluctance he was showing was simply and solely due to her. But why?

She smiled at him. "Well, Mr. Vallender, you have three very eager, would-be guests clamoring around you, have you no answer for us?" She suddenly wanted very much to be invited to Castell Melyn—

"Then you must all come then, of course, if you are so set upon my poor Lady Jacquetta."

Annabel clapped her hands excitedly. "I can scarce wait!"

Richard laughed. "I do not return to my ghost for another two weeks, I fear, but from that moment on you may hunt her to your heart's content."

"*Two* weeks—oh, it sounds like a lifetime."

Chris stretched his long legs. "And I cannot leave London for a week or two myself, my affairs will not permit it."

Mally suddenly remembered her promise to her mother. "Oh, dear, I fear *I* may have to step down after all—"

Annabel's face fell. "But, Mally, you cannot! I should not be permitted to go alone and that would mean my chaperone! Oh, please, don't be so horrid as to decline!"

"But I promised my mother I would return to Llanglyn with her at the end of this week."

Richard turned swiftly toward her. "Your mother still lives in Llanglyn?"

"Yes." She could see a strange expression in his dark eyes again. An anxiety almost— "Perhaps you know her, Mr. Vallender. Her name is Mrs. Olivia Berrisford of Llanglyn Court."

He stared. "She is *your* mother? I confess I had no idea. No idea at all."

Chris looked at him in surprise. "To say that you seem taken aback, Richard, would be to put it somewhat mildly."

Richard laughed shortly. "I *am* taken aback. This makes things a little awkward. Even embarrassing. You see, Chris, Mrs. Berrisford does not approve of me in the slightest. She regards me, I fancy, as the very source of all things doubtful—very definitely a toad of the first order."

"Good heavens," said Annabel, "what *ever* have you been doing?"

Richard looked at Mally. "I take it that your mother has mentioned my name?"

"Yes, Mr. Vallender, and you would indeed seem to be a toad of the first order in her opinion."

"And in yours?"

"No—unless all toads are charming company."

He inclined his head, smiling. "I am quite overcome at your kindness. But, in view of this, if you think you wish to change your mind about visiting—"

Oh, how he wants to keep me out. Mally felt more and more with each second that if he wanted her away from Castell Melyn, then she must do all in her power to thwart him. "I know—I can go to Llanglyn with Mother, stay with her for two weeks, and then when you all go to the castle, I may join you."

Annabel smiled, but then her face fell. "That still means my awful *chaperone!* She will have to drive all the way to Breconshire with me and I could not bear it, I just could not bear it!"

Mally was up to each problem. "Then you shall come to Berrisford Court with me, Annabel. Mother would be *charmed* to have such an important guest, I'm sure." She felt Richard's thoughtful eyes on her and stifled the urge to meet his gaze, for she knew that her own eyes would be uncomfortably triumphant at that moment.

Chris went to bring a decanter and four glasses to the table before them. "It is settled then. In two weeks' time we all sally forth to Castell Melyn. A toast would be in order, I fancy. The Lady Jacquetta, may she materialize and rattle her chains before our wondering eyes!"

Mally raised her glass. "To Lady Jacquetta," she said, and this time she did meet Richard's eyes.

He smiled and raised his glass to her, but he said nothing.

Chapter 11

Mally closed the door of the Green Room behind her with a sigh of relief. Beyond the door she could still hear her mother fussing around over the supervision of the two harassed maids.

"No, gel! That lace must *not* be treated indifferently! Good heavens, how you have managed to cling to your position in this house I shall never *begin* to comprehend! That's a little better. Gently. *Gently!*"

Mally took a long breath and counted slowly to ten. For someone who had rushed to London in an anxious hurry, her mother had managed to pack enough clothing for a whole season! Straightening her dainty lace mobcap, Mally descended the stairs, intent upon the sanctuary of the library.

Someone hammered on the front doors and she paused on the stairs, watching Digby come slowly up from the basement. Who could be calling?

The butler looked down his nose at the dirty boy standing there. "Back door for the likes of you!" he snapped, starting to close the doors.

"Got a message."

"Back door."

"Couldn't give a tinker's, I bin paid." The boy dropped the folded paper he held and ran off, stopping at the foot of the steps to make a rude gesture at the quivering Digby.

Mally continued down the stairs into the hallway. "What is it, Digby?"

"A message, madam, brought by some—some flash-house brat!"

"For me?"

"Yes, madam." The butler glanced at the writing and handed it to her.

Curious, she unfolded the crisp paper, which was marred by the boy's dirty fingerprints.

Mrs. St. Aubrey, I hesitate to write this note, but I feel that perhaps under the circumstances it would be wise for us to meet before you leave for Llanglyn, and most certainly before you come to Castell Melyn. There are matters which should be spoken of between us, as I feel you already know. I shall be riding in the park this morning should you be in agreement with me. Richard Vallender.

Mally folded the paper again very slowly. Matters which should be spoken of? It could only be Maria—"Digby, I wish the barouche to be at the front door in half an hour."

"Yes, madam. Forgive me, but are you still expecting Sir Christopher to dine tonight?"

"Yes, there has been no change in that, Digby."

The butler bowed and she turned to hurry up the stairs, calling for Lucy.

The barouche clattered along the crowded streets where the autumn sun was oddly warm. Bright summery gowns and colors were drawn out by this last brilliance, and as the barouche neared the park, the usual clutter of fashionable drags began to increase in volume. Dry leaves scuttered over the cobbles and grass, and above the gay gold, red, and green, the sky was a clear, endless blue.

Mally toyed with her yellow reticule and glanced down at her white muslin gown. The pearl buttons of her dark brown spencer gleamed against the rich velvet, and for the tenth time she retied the yellow ribbons of her bonnet, wondering if the chenille roses adorning it were looking as excellent as she had thought. She nodded and smiled as someone drove past, raising a hand to her. Again and again she acknowledged acquaintances, but all the while she searched for Richard Vallender. What had he to say to her? Was it another attempt to prevent her from going to Castell Melyn?

She saw him beneath the trees, a tall, lean figure in dull gray velvet and cords. He had not seen her and she saw the way he tapped his top hat against his leg. There was a tautness about him, she felt, and that notion was confirmed at the swiftness with which he turned when the barouche halted beside him.

"Mr. Vallender?"

His eyes went over her and then he smiled. "I trust you were not offended by my action in writing to you, Mrs. St. Aubrey."

She climbed down as he opened the carriage door, and his hand was firm as he helped her.

The autumn leaves seemed to lie in drifts as they walked across the park. "I am not offended, Mr. Vallender, for I agree that we should perhaps speak."

"Of your sister, Maria."

"You speak familiarly of her, sir."

"Because I consider her to be my friend. As I consider myself to be yours—at least, I like to *think* I am yours."

She halted and looked at his lean face. "Come to the point, sir, for I am here at *your* instigation, am I not?"

"Very well. Knowing full well that Maria was betrothed to Thomas Clevely, I more than aided and abetted her friendship with my wife's cousin, Andrew York."

"Your wife's cousin?"

"He was. Mrs. St. Aubrey—oh, dear God, may I call you Mally, for to be polite takes rather a long time."

"I do not know yet whether I wish to be on such intimate terms with you, Mr. Vallender."

"You are splendidly haughty when you wish. I connived at your sister's *affaire* with Andrew, and partly on account of that dabbling on my part, I am very *out* with your mother. Very out."

"That I know, for she is not hesitant in passing her opinion on you, Mr. Vallender."

"No doubt."

"Where is my sister, Mr. Vallender?"

"I don't know."

She looked at him. He was lying, she knew that he was. "Have you brought me here merely to play cat and mouse, sir? Because if you have, then I shall leave you right now."

"In high dudgeon?" He was smiling, and he drew her hand through his arm and walked on. "Mrs. St. Aubrey, I have not brought you here on a fool's errand. It is merely that I wished to admit to you my part in Maria's association with Andrew. I have no desire to be at odds with you over such a matter, for I value my friendship with Chris too much to cross swords with his future wife."

"Mr. Vallender, if Maria put Mr. York before Mr. Clevely, that is her prerogative, and I would not be at odds with anyone over it. But Mr. York is now dead, and my sister has disappeared. So, I must ask myself if you— being so friendly with her that you may term her merely 'Maria' and not 'Miss Berrisford'—know the name of the man she has gone off with?" She halted again and looked up at him. "Do you, Mr. Vallender?"

"I know of no one in your sister's life apart from Andrew York."

"Then why was it that when Dr. Towers came from Castell Melyn and spoke with her, by the next morning she had gone from my mother's house?"

"I know nothing of anything else, Mrs. St. Aubrey." He smiled again with that easy charm which marked everything about him. "It is solely on account of this that there may have been any hesitation on my part over your coming to Castell Melyn, a hesitation which I feel certain you detected."

She kept her eyes firmly on the path ahead and the sun on the grass in the distance. *Was* that his sole reason? He was clever, carefully covering each track, but he planned without the tenacity lent to her by anxiety. She said nothing, waiting to see what reaction her silence brought.

"Mrs. St. Aubrey, if you still feel that you wish to come, then I should be more than delighted, but if you think you would offend your mother—"

He still wants me away from his lair— The conviction was strong and would not be denied. The invitation had been issued—albeit under duress of one sort or another—and it had been accepted. And would continue to be accepted. She turned her head to meet his sharp eyes. "Mr. Vallender, you are laboring under a most certain misapprehension. I am my own commander, not under my mother, and I have given my word to Lady Annabel that we shall come to Castell Melyn. She is looking forward to it so much that I should be a positive beast to deny her now. Unless *you* would prefer me not to come. That would, of course, be entirely different."

A quick light passed through his eyes and he raised her hand to his lips. "Mrs. St. Aubrey, nothing was further from my mind, I assure you. Let us consider the matter closed then, and please forgive my clumsy handling of so delicate a conversation."

"Clumsy? Mr. Vallender, I would not say that you were clumsy, not in the slightest." She smiled innocuously, knowing a sleek satisfaction at his having to hide his annoyance. Short of being outwardly rude, he had done all he could to turn her from her purpose. He knew more about Maria than he was prepared to say, and Mally was determined to find out what that something was. But why was he so concerned to keep her away? She pondered the unease which he had displayed when he realized that she was a Berrisford. His subsequent talk of not wishing to further tread on her mother's toes or of not wishing to be at odds with Chris's future wife was all a screen. There was some other reason for her not to come to Castell Melyn—

They began to walk slowly back toward the barouche and she glanced up at his profile. There was something very attractive about Richard Vallender, something in his dark knowing eyes and quick smile, and the way he moved and spoke; something which would catch the interest of most women— Perhaps even Maria. She walked deep in the drift of her thoughts, glad that the brim of her bonnet hid her face from him. When Andrew York had died, where might Maria turn for comfort? To Richard Vallender?

"What was Andrew York like, Mr. Vallender?"

"Like all the Yorks. He had bright blue eyes and fair hair. And an appealing air of vulnerability."

That's how Mother described him—"What a strange way of describing him. Or are you describing all the Yorks in that last phrase?"

"All of them? Yes. It was her vulnerability which first drew me to Gillian. Her father was strict, cloistering her in that damned house week in and week out. She was pathetically delighted when he relented sufficiently to allow her to drive out with me. It is fatal, Mrs. St. Aubrey, to allow your feelings to have the better of your common sense."

"Your enthusiasm is a little crushing."

"I didn't love her. I felt protective, oh, so very protective—but it wasn't love in the true sense necessary for happiness."

"Poor Gillian."

He smiled enigmatically. "Gillian was never aware of being deceived. You see, she had never known love before and was therefore content with what I gave. But then you do not wish to hear about that. Do you? Never, Mrs. St. Aubrey, make the same mistake—never marry when your heart is less than completely given. It is not worth the heartache."

She stared at him. "I would never make that mistake, Mr. Vallender," she said softly.

"Of course not, I was merely alluding to my own error. Thank you for coming here today—I look forward to enjoying your company again soon at Castell Melyn."

"And I yours. Good day, Mr. Vallender."

"Good day, Mrs. St. Aubrey." He kissed her hand again and then helped her into the barouche.

She did not look back as the barouche drew away into the throng of carriages and horses. The rattle and noise of London was deadened as she stared at the coachman's back. *Never marry when your heart is less than completely given. It is not worth the heartache.* He had guessed. Had she been that obvious then, that after one evening in her company he could put his finger so unerringly on the pulse? She leaned her head back and closed her eyes wearily.

Chapter 12

"But why didn't you tell me about Maria before?" Tenderly Chris put his hand to Mally's cheek, his brown eyes bright in the flickering firelight. The shadows danced over the library and the air was warm.

"I promised Mother, she feared so for Maria's reputation. She was hoping beyond hope that my sister had run away to me here."

"But Maria is with some unknown gentleman, having gone all the way back to Hereford."

"Yes. Mother doesn't know that last piece of information, though. I just wanted to stop her worrying and upsetting herself, and so I glossed over the country gentleman who asked about Maria at the Swan with Two Necks, and refrained from mentioning that the trail led back to Hereford. Oh, it's too bad of my sister, really it is! She hasn't given a single thought to the misery she's causing by her selfishness! One little notelet would have been sufficient."

"Well, it's done now, and when the Clevelys are informed, I fear your sister's name will be maligned from one end of the county to the other."

"I know. I've promised Mother that we will say Maria is with relatives, but we cannot keep that up forever. She just hopes that in the meantime we will hear from my sister."

"I'm surprised at Maria really. Your mother and the late Mrs. Harmon were such close friends, it doesn't really seem like Maria to be so heartless."

"I know. Anyway, whatever the ins and outs of all this, Maria has gone. Oh, Chris, she has been leading a busy life—being betrothed to Thomas, spending too much time in the company of Mr. Vallender's late cousin, and then scurrying off with yet another man. I cannot comprehend her versatility."

Chris smiled. "Well, she must be all right, for she went willingly enough, it would seem. I'll warrant Richard nearly choked when he realized who you were!"

"Yes. Anyway, this morning we met in the park and spoke of it. He doesn't know where Maria is now." Mally stared at the flames as they lapped around a holly log. She couldn't bring herself to tell him about her suspicions concerning Richard Vallender. There was no point anyway, for she had nothing tangible to say, merely a collection of notions and convictions, feelings and intuitions. And he would laugh them away, for he felt warmly toward his old friend—

Chris drew her down to the rug before the fire, stretching forward to pick up the poker and setting the sparks and flames leaping as he plunged it into the heart of the fire. His hair was burnished as he turned to look down at her as she lay beside him.

"Mally, do you *really* think the man at the inn here in London and the man who broke into this house are one and the same?"

"I think so, but I cannot be sure. I just feel that someone else is looking very earnestly for Maria and I am more afraid of that than of anything else in all this."

"There is nothing you can do, you know." He stroked her hair softly, making the little diamond pin holding the curls flash and twinkle in the firelight.

"I know." She caught his hand. Richard Vallender's words echoed around in her head. *Never marry when your heart is less than completely given. It is not worth the heartache*— But she *did* love Chris, and all her fears and doubts were foolish and groundless. When she was with him like this, everything was certain and true. She pulled his fingers to her mouth and kissed them. "I love you, Chris. I was thinking—I shall be twenty-nine on the fifteenth of December. It would be an excellent day to marry, for Lucy says it is always sunshine on my birthday."

He bent down to put his lips over hers. "I would not care if it blew a hurricane, sweetheart. The fifteenth of December it is then."

She put her arms around him and held him close, her eyes closed. He laughed then. "There is a problem though."

"What is it?"

"I have asked Richard to be my best man—I cannot think that your mother will be too pleased."

Nor me, I won't be pleased either— The thought was there. Instant and plain. She did not want Richard Vallender there when she married Chris, standing with his smiling face and inward disapproval of the decision she had made. But she said nothing of the sort as she smiled at Chris. "If you have asked him then that is the end of it."

"The next week or so until I reach Llanglyn will seem like a lifetime. I cannot look forward to your leaving tomorrow."

She laughed quietly. "And then when we *do* meet again we shall all be searching for Annabel's infernal ghost!"

"Poor Annabel, she seems quite in a tizzy over the spectral Lady Jacquetta."

"She is. I've met her twice since that evening and each time she's rattled about the ghost and nothing else. Still—" Mally looked up at him. "Rattling about ghosts is safe enough, isn't it? I think the excitement stems more from the prospect of being under the same roof as you for a while, Chris."

"And does the thought worry you?"

"Any woman who didn't regard Annabel with a healthy respect would be a fool indeed. She's very set on you still, Chris."

He kissed her. "But are *you* set on me, Mally?"

"Yes." She gazed up into his face. "I am."

"Then that is all that matters," he whispered, pulling her even closer. "All that matters in the world."

The fire shifted and the shadows were set spinning and gyrating over the rows of books. Digby knocked at the door, and when his knocks were ignored, he went away again.

Annabel's eyes shone with anticipation as she climbed into the landau, pulling the traveling rug over her knees. "I can hardly believe it! Freedom! No chaperone! No heavy father! Nothing! Just perfect, perfect peace."

"And Chris Carlyon," said Mally dryly.

"Ah, well, even *I* am permitted my hopeless dreams." Annabel smiled.

Mally made herself comfortable and then looked up at the porch of the house where Digby was waiting patiently by the doors for Mrs. Berrisford to come down. The landau lurched as the final trunk was strapped into place.

Annabel leaned forward. "I know that this Lucy person always turns you out to a tee, but are you sure she can cope with me as well? I mean she must be eighty if she's a day!"

"She's not that old, and she's more than able to take care of you, Annabel."

"I note the way you said that. Have you made certain your good lady mother has supped something good and sleepy before this journey, for I warrant I will *die* if she rattles all the way to Llanglyn."

"Then *you* will rattle instead, I suppose."

"I shall console myself with my daydreams."

"You do that small thing."

"Why so acid this morning, didn't you sleep?"

"Not much."

Annabel looked curiously at her, but at that moment Mrs. Berrisford bustled from the porch and down the steps. "Did you pack that necklace, Lucy?"

Lucy tied her mantle firmly beneath her chin and spoke wearily. "Yes, Mrs. Berrisford."

"And the pattens I brought just in case?"

"Yes, Mrs. Berrisford."

"And—"

"I packed everything, Mrs. Berrisford. *Everything*."

Annabel huddled further in the traveling rug and groaned dramatically. Mrs. Berrisford clambered in and searched immediately for the warmed brick to put her feet on. Then she gathered together a mound of rugs and furs and packed herself carefully under layer after layer.

"There," she said at last, "now I shall be quite comfortable. Good morning, Lady Annabel."

"Good morning, Mrs. Berrisford." Annabel smiled sweetly.

Mrs. Berrisford wriggled a little more, and Lucy still waited patiently on the pavement for all the squirming to cease so that she too could take her place. "Marigold," said Mrs. Berrisford suddenly, "I do think that the new name for the house is splendid. Such a touching remembrance of dear Daniel."

"Yes, Mother."

Mrs. Berrisford sighed. "Two years ago this month. Oh, dear, it only seems like yesterday sometimes."

"I know."

Annabel glanced at Mally. "Still, Mally, it is all *past* now, isn't it?"

"Of course." Mally avoided Annabel's gaze.

Lucy climbed in and settled herself carefully in the small place Mrs. Berrisford had left. Mrs. Berrisford looked disapprovingly at her daughter. "Yes, it is all past now and there is Sir Christopher. Which brings me to the disgracefully late hour that gentleman left this house last night. Four o'clock in the morning! What *will* be said of you, that's what I must worry over."

Mally smiled. "Let them say what they will, for I'll be an honest woman on the fifteenth of December."

Annabel's eyes flinched, but her smile hardly faltered. "I congratulate you, Mally."

Mrs. Berrisford beamed. "A date at last! Splendid. Oh, now I can begin to plan everything—oh, how excellent, something to take my poor mind away from all the woes and worries of the last weeks."

Annabel looked out of the carriage as the team pulled away from Vimiero House, and Mally thought she could see tears glistening in her green eyes.

Chapter 13

Llanglyn dreamed in its Welsh march valley, a sleepy market town which for centuries had guarded the shallow ford over the rushing waters of the Afon Glyn which in this one place widened and lost its tumbling force. The dark gray houses and cottages huddled on the eastern bank, ringed here and there still by the remains of the medieval walls and crowned by the tall spire of St. Crispin's. The river sparkled in the sunlight as the landau swayed along the road from Hereford, passing beneath a tracery of autumn trees which dropped dark, clean shadows on the dusty track.

Away to the west, across the river and high on the breast of Long Mountain, rose the silhouette of Castell Melyn, and beyond that the wild, beautiful ruggedness of the Black Mountains themselves, cloud-shadowed and bright against the blue skies. The yellow castle rose above its park of trees and browsing deer, a muddle of towers and battlements which still, even now, looked sturdy enough to withstand any attacking enemy. Mally followed the line of the curving lane which led down from the castle, the only way in and out of the fortress. It vanished at last into the thick trees of the lower woods, but Mally knew that it meandered toward the town, deep between its high banks and hedges until it joined the road by the ford, and by the ivy-covered walls and buildings of Llanglyn Court. She leaned to look across the ford and at last she saw the old courthouse, standing alone and splendid on the rising land beyond the meadows edging the river.

"There it is, Annabel. Journey's end."

"And not before time. Sweet Lord, I ache everywhere—would that I could fall asleep as easily as Lucy and your mother." She nodded at the two sleeping shapes opposite.

Mrs. Berrisford's head wobbled from side to side with each lurch the landau made on the rutted road, and occasionally she gave an indelicate snore which caused Annabel to grit her teeth. But at least it was preferable to the cannonade of excited chattering with which Mrs. Berrisford had assailed them on the first day of the journey. Lucy's head nodded on her chest, her mobcap falling forward over her face so that Mally knew that when she awoke she would not be able to see a thing.

Annabel watched the golden-leaved trees through the window. "Everything out here seems more colorful, doesn't it? The green is greener and the blue bluer, if you know what I mean."

"Yes, everything is more out here. The winter is colder, the weather worse, the snow deeper, earlier, and longer-lasting."

"Don't spoil my enjoyment, Mally—at least, what's left of it." Annabel glanced slyly at her. "I hope it snows on the fifteenth of December, I hope it snows and snows and snows."

"Thank you."

"Don't mention it. Damn you. Oh, why is it my lot in life to love Chris? All I can assume is that in a previous life I must have had one long and exquisite a time of it. Would that I could only remember it!"

"Reincarnation as well as ghosts? You will never cease to surprise me."

"Well, why not ghosts? Mm?"

"You'll tell me next that you believe in fairies too. And werewolves, and bugaboos."

"If I knew any itinerant bugaboos I'd whistle them over to dispose of you, Mrs. St. Aubrey."

Mally laughed. "That's what I like about you, Annabel, you're such a *friend!* When you cease to say such dreadful things to me then I shall *know* you're up to something devious."

The landau turned on the edge of the town and splashed across the ford toward the courthouse. Ivy covered the ancient walls, the leaves flapping in the breeze which swept down from the mountains. The small slit windows facing out toward the town looked unfriendly, like tiny, sharp eyes peering from a shaggy face; on the inside, windows overlooking the enclosed courtyard were elegant and latticed, more homely and welcoming.

The coachman steered the tired team beneath the gatehouse and into the shadows. The hooves and wheels clattered on the cobbles, the sound echoing around the gallery surrounding the entire courtyard, and two grooms ran to attend to the horses as Mally climbed down to stand looking fondly around at her old home.

The pigeons stirred in the dovecote over the gatehouse, the sun falling on their feathers and making them almost unbearably white. Rooks grumbled in the elm trees lining the lane beside the house, rising in a black cloud as something disturbed them. Their angry, raucous voices were sudden and grating. And well remembered. She looked up at the gallery and the soft colored stonework. Nothing ever changed here; surely a fourteenth-century nobleman could step out from the great hall at any moment—

But it was no fourteenth-century nobleman who emerged from the first-floor room, it was a thin, red-headed woman in a clean white apron and gray dress.

"Miss Mally! Oh, Miss Mally, how good it is to see you again."

"Hello, Pattie. Mother? Lucy? Come on, wake up, we've arrived." She leaned in through the door again and shook her mother's arm.

Pattie's shoes sounded loud on the old wooden staircase leading down from the gallery, and she was blinking back the tears as she ran to hug Mally. "Oh, Miss Mally, you look grand, truly you do! Did you—?" Her voice died away as she saw Annabel stepping down. "Oh, *Duw*, for a moment I thought it was Miss Maria."

"No, Pattie."

"Well, come on inside and I'll make a good pot of Pekoe. I've been baking and baking all day since your letter arrived this morning, and I've been making jam with the late blackberries. Oh, there's been such a crop this year."

Mally remained in the courtyard when the others had gone up to the gallery and into the great hall. The team had been unharnessed and the landau stood alone, its doors still open. She took a long breath. There was a hint of dampness in the air, dampness and bracken. And blackberry jam. She crossed toward a narrow arched alley through which she could see the sloping lawns sweeping up from the back of the house.

Bright-berried rowans lined the edges of the grounds, darkened here and there by glossy dark green holly bushes. The ash tree had shed most of its leaves and they still lay on the grass where they had fallen. Shielding her eyes against the slowly setting sun, she looked up toward the castle. It was three miles away, black and solid against the skyline, and she was conscious of a quickening of her pulses as she looked at the stark shape. Why was Richard Vallender so anxious to keep her away?

The sun was dazzling and she had to look away. She crossed the lawns toward the crumbling wall which bordered the narrow lane to the castle. An uncontrolled bramble hung over from the grounds, trailing its thorny strands almost to the rutted mud where recent wheels and horses had passed. Sheep bleated in the fields on the other side of the lane, although she could not see them for the wild clouds of old man's beard draping the hedge in drifts of gray and white. As Mally sat on the low wall, the rooks were just settling back in the elms again, grumbling together in that way rooks have.

There was a robin on the sundial by the lily pool. She had sat here, in this very place, all those years ago when Daniel had proposed to her. And the water lilies had been so fine that year— Would she ever know such happiness again? Was it even possible to love again like that?

She jumped as someone put a hand on her shoulder. "Annabel! Don't creep up on me like that!"

"Creep? I strode across that grass like an infantryman! I have been dispatched to bring you to your good hot Pekoe."

"I marvel that anyone had the *temerity* to dispatch you anywhere." The past was slipping away again. The robin had gone from his perch, and the October breeze was rippling the dark waters of the pool.

Annabel leaned over to look at the lane. "Does this lead up to my nest of ghosties and bugaboos?"

"Yes. The only way in and out of Castell Melyn."

"That doesn't seem very clever planning on some warlord's part, does it? I mean, one narrow way like this? Ideal for ambush. Or siege."

"It wasn't always the only way. The last owner before Mr. Vallender enclosed the huge park you can see, and he closed all the other lanes except this one. He built a very impressive gateway and lodge, you see, and was determined that all his guests should drive through and marvel at it. Lucy told me all about it—her husband used to be the gardener up there. It's a few years ago now."

Annabel shivered. "It's getting colder with each minute. Let's go in."

As Mally stood, she heard a horse coming slowly up the lane from the bottom road, and she turned to see who it was. An old man on a skewbald mare came into view. He was huddled in a voluminous woolen cloak and had a wide-brimmed hat pulled down as far over his ears as he could manage. He looked puzzled as he stared up the winding lane which led away into the trees ahead. With some difficulty he doffed the hat and looked up at Mally.

"Noswaith da," he said politely.

"Good evening, sir," replied Mally.

"Forgive my impertinence in addressing you, but I think that this cannot be the road to Hereford. Turn right at the Llanglyn ford they said, but this seems too narrow and little used."

"You turn after crossing the ford, then you will be right for Hereford."

"Thank you, thank you kindly. But I have traveled too slowly, I fear, and there is little chance that I will reach my destination today. Is there a reputable hostelry in Llanglyn?"

"The Three Feathers, in the market square. You cannot miss it. Jasper Turney is the landlord and he keeps an excellent house."

He pulled the hat on again and began to turn the mare, and suddenly Annabel caught Mally's arm. "What's that? Listen."

It was the thundering of hooves, followed by the violent splashing of the ford as whoever it was rode at such a rate that they set the angry rooks flapping and wheeling again.

"They're coming up the lane!" cried Mally, hearing the

definite slowing of the hoofbeats as the riders negotiated the sharp turn. "They're going too fast!"

"Arglwydd mawr!" whispered the old gentleman, looking apprehensively in the direction of the sound as he tried to urge the placid mare to safety. But she remained where she was, stubbornly across the narrow lane. The three horsemen barely had time to rein in, the excited horses capering and plunging, sending dust spinning around them.

"Jasper Turney and Brew Darril," murmured Mally to Annabel, "and the young one with the freckles is Jasper's brother Jacob."

"Mine host of the Three Feathers would seem to be in a fine fury," said Annabel, shaking a little as she realized how close the old gentleman had come to being ridden down.

"He's very opinionated and loud-mouthed, considers himself to be the spokesman for the whole of Breconshire on every conceivable subject."

Young Jacob had difficulty with his horse. He was only seventeen and his face was pale and nervous, his tongue passing quickly over his lower lip. "It en't 'im, Jasper! It en't 'im after all!"

"I can see, our Jacob!"

Mally leaned over the wall. "What is the meaning of all this, Mr. Turney?"

He glanced up in surprise, snatching off his dusty top hat. His bearded face was broad and sly and his blue eyes clear and sharp. "It en't nothing, Miss Mally."

"That is not how it seemed when you careered so dangerously up here a moment ago, nearly killing this gentleman in the process. Incidentally, he is a prospective customer for your inn—which *I* wouldn't be now in his shoes!"

The old man looked uncomfortable. *This* ruffian was the landlord of the Three Feathers? He cleared his throat.

Brew's thin, dry face was surly. "I thought as it was the same 'orse."

"An' you knowed what thought done, an' all!"

"Well, there en't that many colored 'orses as comes up this way, now, is there, Jasper?" Brew prepared to defend himself.

Mally was curious. "Are you in the habit of pursuing every rider of skewbald horses, Mr. Darril?"

"Only them as comes this way."

"Why?"

"Brew!" Jasper spoke shortly. "Time en't right."

Annabel stepped closer to the wall. "On the contrary, Mr. Turney, it would seem to me that the time is perfect for an explanation. After all, it is hardly the done thing, is it—galloping like fiends after innocent passersby? One would imagine pursuit of that kind to be the prerogative of those outside the law."

He stared up at her, his mouth open. "And who might you be, then?"

"I am Lady Annabel Murchison, daughter of the Earl of Hartmore, and I am awaiting your reply, Mr. Turney."

Jacob Turney's eyes widened. " 'Ere, Jasper—"

"All right, all right, Jacob. Well, my lady, we chases after one particular colored horse. The one as belongs to the murderin' devil as killed poor Mrs. Harmon in her bed some weeks back. That negro killed 'er, right enough, no matter *what* Towers do say. Him and Vallender stands together and looks all innocent as says that there feller couldn't 'ave done it—well, we knows different."

"Then I suggest, Mr. Turney," said Annabel, "that you point out these matters to someone in authority rather than take the law into your own hands."

"The law's blind and deaf to justice round 'ere, my lady. That black one was seen, seen by more'n one, an' all. But when folks like Vallender says otherwise, then there's no one will thwart 'em. But we'll get en in th'end, don't you fret. That old biddy will be revenged."

He turned his horse and kicked it savagely. Brew and Jacob followed him and the lane was quiet again but for the old gentleman on his patient horse. He cleared his throat again. "I believe—on reflection—that perhaps I will ride on a little way yet. Yes. Indeed. *Nos da.*" He doffed his hat and then persuaded the mare to move on again. "Come on, Esyllt, that's my girl."

Mally and Annabel watched him until he passed from sight. "I wouldn't be happy sleeping under your Mr. Turney's roof either," said Annabel at last.

"He's hardly *my* Mr. Turney."

"Are those three ruffians a sample of the inhabitants of Llanglyn? They sounded most un-Welsh."

"Hereford—and Mother will tell you that *that* is a place of origin worse than any, bar London."

Annabel smiled. "Toffee-nosed woman, your mother. Well, I came to seek excitement up at the castle, but I rather fancy there is more going on down here in the valley. Don't you?"

"Come on, the sun's gone and that tea will be cold. And Mother will grizzle at it being wasted."

As they walked back to the house, Mally glanced up at Castell Melyn for a last time. A solitary light burned in one of the towers, winking slightly in the gathering darkness.

Chapter 14

"Come through into the kitchens, my dears," said Pattie. "It's warmer here."

They pushed open a studded wooden door and the smell of blackberry jam was immediately stronger. Warmed jars stood on the scrubbed table and another pan was bubbling slowly on the range which had been installed earlier that summer. Pattie polished a last cup and set it carefully on the dainty blue and white saucer. "There, I've kept the pot hot."

"Where's Mother?"

"Gone to her bed—Lucy's attending to her."

"Pattie, what's been going on here since Mrs. Harmon died?" asked Mally, watching the tea as Pattie poured it.

"Going on?"

"You know what I mean. Lady Annabel and I have just witnessed an incident which is alarming in its implications, to say the least. Jasper Turney—"

"Oh, that one! Ne'er-do-well. Him and his crony Brew Darril. And now they're taking young Jacob in tow as well—it's not right, not right at all. *Duw*, they're the worst pair of poaching scoundrels this side of Hereford.

Always conniving at something outside the law. And now, since Mrs. Harmon's death, what with Dr. Towers standing up to them like that, they're setting about—about—"

"A witch hunt?" asked Annabel.

Pattie put the teapot down and placed the woolen cosy over it. "Well, we all *know* that that black man was in Llanglyn that night, and I *saw* him out in the lane myself. Whatever I might think of Jasper, he *is* right about this, and justice isn't being done. No, it most certainly isn't."

Mally lifted a cloth which covered fresh-baked raspberry buns. "Well, Pattie, if they do lynch this poor fellow from Castell Melyn, then the law will catch up with them all right. It will achieve nothing."

"Miss Mally, feelings are running very high around these parts. Those up at Castell Melyn are not liked, and only the catching of the murderer will stop it all."

"And Dr. Towers *insists* that the man could not have been in Llanglyn?"

"Yes. Sticks to it like a fly to treacle."

"Oh, Pattie, Dr. Towers would hardly—"

Pattie sniffed. "Him and that there Mr. Vallender are as thick as thieves. Towers would say anything to please him, you mark my words."

Annabel raised her eyebrows. "Our Mr. Vallender certainly manages to put people's backs up, doesn't he, Mally? Mm? He must have brought the absolute *end* in wooden spoons with him from America."

Pattie pushed the tea toward Mally. "Mrs. Berrisford says as you are going to stay up at the castle next week or the week after."

"Yes. Lady Annabel is filled with a desire to come face to face with the wraith of Lady Jacquetta."

"That old tale! There's never been a ghost up there, never in all these years. But Miss Mally, don't go. Stay back here, where it's—"

"Safe? Pattie, we are going there. *I* will not pass judgment on anyone at the castle. And I regard Mr. Vallender as my friend—indeed, he is to be the best man when I marry Sir Christopher. Now, you can hardly expect me to join in the general howling, can you?"

Pattie took a long breath. "No, Miss Mally. Let's talk of something else then, shall we? Here, I baked these for you, they were always your favorite, weren't they? And Miss Maria's." She glanced nervously at Annabel, for she had been told not to speak of Maria in front of the guest.

But Annabel was looking at the raspberry buns. "Those look quite delicious. But, I had the dismaying experience of discovering this morning that my favorite spencer is somewhat tight. Get thee behind me, raspberry buns!" She got to her feet. "I shall take myself to that genuine fifteenth-century fourposter you promised me, Mally. I trust only that our forebears appreciated the finer points of *soft* beds."

Mally grinned. "Soft? Good heavens, no. That would have been considered namby-pamby."

Annabel smiled sweetly. "I know—hard bed, hard head. Ah, me."

Pattie smoothed her apron. "Don't you pay any attention to her, Lady Annabel. That is the finest bed in the marches, the very finest."

When Annabel had gone, Mally took a bun. "Pattie, now that we are alone, perhaps we can talk about Maria."

"Mrs. Berrisford was telling me what you discovered. I cannot understand it, Miss Mally, for she loved that Mr. York. Oh, she didn't tell the half of it to your poor mother, but she told me. She loved him so much, she was going to send Mr. Clevely's ring back and everything. She'd made up her mind. In fact, on the night of the murder, she had gone to meet Mr. York to tell him that she had accepted him."

"Mr. York *proposed* to her?"

"Oh, yes. Yes, indeed."

"Did you meet him, Pattie?"

"Yes." Pattie looked uncomfortable. "I don't know whether I should tell you all this, for if your mother found out how I'd helped Miss Maria, I'd be thrown out of this house, I know that I would."

"Pattie, I won't rattle on you, the very idea! What was he like?"

Pattie sat down and poured herself a cup of tea, and then sat back, looking fondly at the black cat curled up on the rocking chair. "Oh, such a nice young man. He talked strangely, mind, but then he was an American. And he treated her like she was procelain. *Such* manners."

"Mother speaks of him as being totally unsuitable."

"He was virtually penniless, that's why. He was only with Mr. Vallender because of that. Mind, *he* liked Mr. Vallender, always defended him if anything detrimental was said. Miss Maria liked him too, spoke most strongly for him, she did. Oh, when I think of how happy she was, Miss Mally, I just *cannot* believe that all the time she was meeting someone else. It just isn't possible."

Maria had liked Richard Vallender. Mally found herself wondering again about the enigmatic Mr. Vallender.

"Pattie, the day before Maria left Dr. Towers came to speak with her."

"Yes. She was out there in the gardens, breaking her heart over Mr. York. We couldn't get any sense out of her and we were so afraid that she'd seen Mrs. Harmon's murderer or something—" Pattie took a long breath. "But, then the doctor came and whatever it was that he said to her halted the tears right enough. There was—oh, I don't know—an *air* about her for the rest of that day."

"An air?"

"Yes, you know, an excitement. And then, when we rose from our beds the next day, she'd gone. Just like that. No note. Nothing at all. We knew she'd gone properly when we found her clothes had been taken as well. Not all of them, just enough to fit in that leather handcase she had."

"And then you heard that Mr. York was dead."

Pattie's eyes filled with tears. "Yes. And coming on top of Maria going, Mrs. Harmon being murdered an' all, it was such a shock. I liked him, Miss Mally, and he'd have made a splendid husband for her. She did so love him." Pattie sniffed. "Which is why I will *not* believe she has gone away with another man, this fellow with the phaeton."

Mally put down the bun slowly, a new thought creeping horribly into her mind. "Pattie, you don't think— I mean, if Maria ran away and *then* Mr. York was found."

Pattie put down her cup and saucer abruptly. "Oh, *no*, Miss Mally. No, no, we cannot believe any such thing. Don't even say it. I beg of you."

"Then it *had* crossed your mind, hadn't it?"

"No!"

Mally fell silent, poking the crumbs of the bun around the plate with a thoughtful finger. Pattie watched her. "She loved him, Miss Mally, she loved him and *nothing* will change my mind on that. She had nothing to do with his death."

The clock on the mantlepiece ticked softly in the quiet, and the cat stood, arching its back as it stretched. Then it turned around on the cushion several times and settled down to sleep again.

Mally sat back. "I think that that animal has good sense. Bed would seem to be in order, don't you think?"

"Miss Mally, do *you* believe Miss Maria has eloped?"

"I don't know, Pattie. But I *do* know one thing—tomorrow I intend taking myself across to Llanglyn to pay a visit to Dr. Nathaniel Towers. I would very much like to know what he had to say to her the day before she left, wouldn't you?"

"He might tell you, Miss Mally, but he denied saying anything much to her when your mother and I faced him with it. You ask him, Miss Mally. And we'll see."

Chapter 15

The rain streamed down, tamping on the cobbled square and running in rivulets down the street toward the church. Even the Three Feathers was quiet and deserted, its sign creaking as it swayed in the icy wind which howled down from the mountains.

Mally climbed down from the landau and hurried toward the steps leading between George Cunningworth's grocery store and the livery stable. Her pattens were awkward and she could not go very quickly, so that in no time the rain had soaked through her pelisse to dampen her shivering shoulders. She had climbed halfway up toward the doctor's rambling old cottage, when she turned to look back. Mrs. Harmon's house stood opposite. The curtains were tightly drawn, and there was no smoke from its chimneys. It looked empty and forlorn.

Mally hurried on up the steps and through the green painted gate of the doctor's cottage. She knocked, pressing beneath the tiny porch to get out of the rain as much as she could. To the left of the cottage was the upper portion of the churchyard. The wind whispered coldly through the yew trees, and the rain glistened on the gravestones. She looked toward the church itself. Daniel's grave was just visible, the gray marble cross quite plain and uncluttered.

Quickly she turned her back toward it, holding her breath to force away the wave of sadness which swept immediately over her. But before she turned she noticed the other grave close by. Also plain and without any fancy trappings. Was that Andrew York's grave? Mother had said it was but ten feet away from Daniel's—

The door opened suddenly. Dr. Towers ushered her in. "I'd forgotten my housekeeper had gone to visit her sister, Mrs. St. Aubrey, and I sat there waiting for her to show you in. I saw you come up the steps. Come and sit by the fire. There now, let me take that wet pelisse."

She bent to unstrap the wooden pattens, and immediately felt at least two inches shorter. She was still shivering when she held her cold hands out to the roaring fire. Copper pans and bowls gleamed in the hearth, and a bowl of dark red chrysanthemums filled the air with their sharp scent. She looked quickly away from them.

She watched the doctor as he went to a cupboard to take out two glasses and a decanter. His periwig was freshly powdered, and its black satin bow as perky and flouncy as ever. He prided himself on his wig-bows. His brocade waistcoat was his one salute to fashion, for it was crimson and was quite the most splendid Mally had seen outside London. His buckled shoes clumped on the red-raddled floor as he brought the glasses and wine to a low table.

"A glass of Malmsey, Mrs. St. Aubrey—I take it this is a social and not a professional visit."

"Some Malmsey would go down very well, Dr. Towers. But surely I am not to be called Mrs. St. Aubrey in so stern a fashion. When I was a child you called me Miss Mally, and I see no reason for that to change, do you?"

He smiled. "Soon it will be Lady Carlyon—I thought

perhaps a little healthy respect now would not come amiss. However, as you say, it was always Miss Mally, and Miss Mally it shall be again. Now then, what brings you to me so swiftly after your arrival at the courthouse? It was only yesterday evening, so I understand."

"Yes." She sat in the proffered chair and sipped the wine. "Dr. Towers, I think you probably know what I am about to ask you."

"What I said to your sister which made her leave? Yes, I thought that that would be the reason you are here. Well, I will be honest, I cannot remember what I said. In fact, I don't think I said *anything* of importance."

She studied his wrinkled face. "Then it will surely be the first conversation you have taken part in which you cannot recall *months* later, let alone days or weeks."

"Nonetheless, Miss Mally, I cannot remember this one." He met her gaze steadily.

"So, you know nothing about it at all."

"Nothing."

She sipped the wine again. "And nothing about her association with the late Mr. York?"

"I know *of* it, yes."

"And not merely because of your friendship with Mr. Vallender, I take it. Dr. Towers, my sister is with child, isn't she?"

He exhaled slowly. "That is asking me to divulge facts about another patient, Miss Mally."

"You don't have to divulge it, I can see it in your face. Maria is expecting Mr. York's child."

"I have admitted nothing."

"Point taken."

"Please don't say it like that, Miss Mally, for it *would* be wrong of me to say anything. It is hardly my place to utter a word, is it?"

"Perhaps not, but then we don't know where Maria is or who she is with, do we? Unless—do *you* know?"

"No."

"And you also know nothing about someone *else* who is seeking her whereabouts?"

He would not look at her. "No."

"Then perhaps I shall soon find someone who *can* help me. At the castle when I go there to stay."

He sat forward. "You are going to *stay* there?"

"Yes. At Mr. Vallender's kind invitation."

"I—I did not realize you knew him so well."

She thought that the doctor was very taken aback, although he was striving to hide it. "I do not know him well, Dr. Towers, but Sir Christopher does. Sir Christopher, Mr. Vallender, and Daniel were close friends in their youth."

He sat back again, toying with the stem of his glass. "I had not realized. I knew that Mr. Vallender and Daniel were once friends, of course, and that that was the reason for buying Castell Melyn."

"We met him when out driving in Hyde Park."

"How—fortuitous."

"Perhaps. We shall see, shall we not? Well, I will take my leave of you now, Dr. Towers. Has it stopped raining?" She went to the window and raised the lace curtain.

Outside, the rain still streamed down relentlessly. Over the roof of the grocery store in the street below, she could see Mrs. Harmon's house. "I hope they catch the man who murdered that old lady," she said, dropping the curtain again.

"Oh, they will, Miss Mally. In the end they will."

"You know that there is a virtual witch hunt for that Negro, don't you?"

"Yes, I could hardly remain unaware of it."

"You *are* sure about him, aren't you? Absolutely sure?"

"Yes, Miss Mally. Poor Abel is wrongly accused. He did not murder Mrs. Harmon."

She took her pelisse from the hook in the hall. "Does Mr. Vallender know what's going on here?"

"No, it was relatively peaceful when he left to go to London."

"What happened then? What started it all?"

"The vicar, I suppose. He sent word to the army fort in Abergavenny, asking them to come and arrest Abel. They came, out there in the market square on market day. There couldn't have been a more attentive audience had they planned it. The officer in charge came up here, to ask me again if I knew Abel had not done it. I said that Abel could not have left his sick bed that night. The officer accepted my word and took his men back to Abergavenny. To say that my name is disliked in Llanglyn at the moment, Miss Mally, would surely be to put it excessively mildly. They blame me, and Mr. Vallender, for keeping a murderer free. That is how they see it."

"But you know different?"

"Yes, I know different. Abel is not a murderer."

"But he *was* in Llanglyn that night, wasn't he?" she said softly, turning to face him as she tied her bonnet ribbons again.

"No."

He opened the door and the sound of the wind and rain blustered into the low-ceilinged hallway. Mally strapped on the pattens. "Dr. Towers, when you avoid my eyes so often, as you have done this morning, and when Pattie says *she* saw him, then I know I would prefer to believe that *she* is the one who is speaking the truth.

"Miss Mally, we have been friends for too long to let anything rankle. Abel did not do anything to Mrs. Harmon, he was too ill to leave his bed. Those who think they saw him are mistaken."

She stepped out into the rain, her pattens sounding oddly hollow as she went down the path.

Chapter 16

"There!" Annabel arranged the ribbons at the throat of her gown and stepped back to admire the effect in the mirror. "I am ready to sally forth!"

Mally stared at her, from the velvet roses topping her jaunty emerald green hat, to the elegant frilled green pelisse and flounced muslin walking dress. The picture was completed by shiny patent slippers peeping from beneath the hem.

"You look fit for a drive in Hyde Park maybe, but not for a visit to Llanglyn on market day! You'll be like a butterfly in a bees' nest."

"That, my dear Mally, is the intention. I have moldered in this house for more than a week. Positively *moldered!* It has rained ever since we arrived and now, at long last, it has stopped. And I intend stepping out looking my very best. All the clod-hoppers can gape, if they wish. Perhaps they know nothing of ladies of quality."

"Your eyes will cross if you look down your nose much more, my lady."

Annabel smiled quickly. "Well, I didn't come here to talk recipes, learn to crochet, or to help bottle jam!"

Mally burst out laughing. "And I am assured that you are proving quite excellent at such homely matters! Your crochet, I am told, is rather presentable."

"Silence, *chienne!* What would the *haut ton* say should a whisper of this get out? I thought horsetails were attached to animals, but it seems they grow in ditches and you scour pans with them. I'll warrant it's one of the wonders of nature." Annabel looked at her hands. "That Pattie of yours did it deliberately. Look at my hands, they're quite *pink!*"

"Pattie did what?"

"Looked witheringly at me and said that I wouldn't be able to manage the roast-pan. It was a gauntlet, waved under my nose and tossed disdainfully to the ground!"

"You should have known better than to let her get under your skin like that."

"She thinks I am disgustingly useless."

"And so you are. But very, *very* decorative. You'll find some pattens in that cupboard, by the way."

"Pattens? I'm not wearing those clumsy things."

"Then get muddy, wet feet."

"Patent needs no pattens."

"You will spoil those slippers, for Llanglyn's mud is master of spoiling anything, given the chance."

"Pattens would not become this toggery." Annabel admired her lovely reflection again.

"Very well, look ridiculous with muddy feet instead, but don't say you weren't warned."

Annabel watched Mally strapping on pattens. "You aren't really going to go out with those on your feet are you?"

"Yes."

"Oh, well, perhaps I will as well, but it will look quite *desperate,* I just know it will. Still, at least no one who matters will see me."

Mally looked up. "Meaning Chris, presumably."

"Yes. *Is* there anyone else who matters? Oh, the Prince of Wales, perhaps. I can't call anyone else to mind."

Mally laughed. "The Prince only *perhaps?* I'm sure he'd take to his bed for a month if he heard."

"Do you think Chris will come soon? And Mr. Vallender? I so want to get up there." Annabel looked from the tiny window and up the hills to the distant castle.

"Any day now, I should think. Chris's business was completed two days ago, I know, for he said that his last meeting was then. It could be that he will be here when we return, who can say?"

Annabel looked anew at the pattens. "Perhaps I *will* leave them off then—"

"Oh, for goodness' sake! Chris is more likely to think you ridiculous if you *don't* wear them, if his opinion is so very important to you. Now then, where are my gloves? Right. Are we ready?"

"I believe so."

Down in the kitchen Mrs. Berrisford and Pattie were surveying a rather battered cookery book. Mrs. Berrisford put her spectacles away. "Well, I don't know, Pattie—the writing's faded so much I really cannot *begin* to guess what that fourth ingredient is. Perhaps it would be prudent to forget Grandmama's excellent dill cake and bake something we are sure of."

"Yes," agreed Pattie, "that would be best, I think."

Mally smiled. "It's only the vicar's wife coming to tea, Mother, not the dreaded Mrs. Clevely."

"Oh, heaven forbid!" Mrs. Berrisford put her hands to her cheeks. "Don't even *mention* that woman. Where is Lady Annabel?"

"Waiting in the barouche. I just came in to see if you wanted me to bring anything back from town."

Mrs. Berrisford looked anxious. "What am I to say to Mrs. Jones this afternoon, Marigold? She is about to ask about Maria, and I do not know that I can lie to *her*."

"Then tell her the truth."

"I cannot."

"Then tell her a fib. You must do one or the other. Or look straight through her when she asks. Now then, what shall I purchase for you?"

"I—I made a list somewere. Oh, yes, here it is. Now you make sure George Cunningworth doesn't fob you off with poor quality—I don't know how much your soft London life has made you forget—"

"Nothing of importance, Mother, nothing of importance. Good-bye, then."

"Good-bye, Marigold."

The barouche rattled down toward the ford. The Afon Gwyn was full and swift after the rain, and the coachman teased his nervous team forward very slowly.

Annabel ran her fingers over the drab velvet upholstery. "I wondered that your mother kept *two* fine carriages, but perhaps this one is not so fine after all."

"The landau comes out on high days and holy days. In between it is wrapped in sheets and put away in a corner of the stables. This old barouche is for general journeys around here, in and out of Llanglyn and so on."

"But the dreaded Mrs. Clevely I have heard mentioned would rate the landau, no doubt?"

"Yes."

"I understand your sister is to marry her son."

"Yes."

"Mally, whenever your sister's name is mentioned, I cannot help noticing how reticent everyone suddenly becomes. I have been listening and paying good attention, so there is no point, you know. Your mother's voice carries from one end of the gallery to the other—and back again sometimes. Maria has run away, hasn't she?"

"You *have* been busy listening, haven't you?"

"A week of rain—there had to be *something* beyond homely pursuits." Annabel smiled.

"Maria has eloped, it would seem."

"And not with her fiancé?"

"Not with him."

"And now she is somewhere, you don't know where, with someone, you don't know who?"

"Yes."

The barouche lurched out of the ford again and the team were brought up to a better pace, their hooves clattering smartly on the flat stones laid on this part of the road.

Annabel leaned out to survey the mud ahead. "Oh, my *Lord!* That isn't mud, it's molasses!"

"I told you."

"I wonder you Llanglyners aren't born with webbed feet!"

The market square was crowded and the noise was tremendous as the stallkeepers shouted their wares. Plump country women carrying hen baskets and fruit baskets walked slowly between the rows of stalls or stopped to talk together in groups. The barouche came to a standstill by a pie stall, and Annabel gazed around. The Hellfire stagecoach was just pulling out of the Three Feathers, team jingling and horn sounding.

"Last calling! Last calling for Hereford!"

Annabel shuddered. "Who could travel in that thing! And look at them? Piled inside like grapes to be pressed."

"Not everyone has various carriages from which to choose, Annabel."

Some loose chickens fluttered from the hooves of the coach's team, scattering in all directions as the horn sounded suddenly. Some penned goats set up a frantic bleating to add to the cacophony, pushing and straining against the hurdles restraining them. A dog began to bark, snapping at the hooves until the driver's whip lashed close to its tail, when it immediately retreated to the safety of a stall.

"Come on, Mally," said Annabel briskly, "let's get down and inspect the stalls. I've never been to a market before."

"Oh, yes you have. Almack's."

They visited George Cunningworth's store, checking each item purchased with great care, including the close examination of the quality of the flour.

"That there flour *en't* 'dulterated, there *en't nothing* in that bag 'ceptin' good grain. *Dam,* I'd swear it on a stack of Bibles, so help me I would!"

"You had better be being honest, Mr. Cunningworth."

"As the day is long, Mrs. St. Aubrey. As the day is long."

Annabel sniffed. "Mm—the evening's *are* drawing in, aren't they?"

"That flour is—"

"We know. Good, pure grain." Annabel dipped her fingers in it. "It's *too* fine and white, isn't it? There's no mill yet that can get it like that. Come, Mr. Cunningworth, you bring the real wheat flour, and we'll forget this poor stuff."

He scowled, snatching the offending bag from the counter and muttering beneath his breath. *"Gast Saesneg!"*

Annabel raised a haughty eyebrow. "Well, *really!* If I am an English one of those, sir, *you* are a *cnaf Cymreig!"*

Mally stared at her. "I had no idea you were so knowledgeable."

"One of the interminable lessons learned this past week at Pattie's knee. When she recovered from the shock of a lady asking how to be rude in Welsh, she was more than obliging."

George thumped a new bag on the counter without a

word. Annabel smiled sweetly and put it in Mally's basket. "Thank you, my man."

Outside Mally burst into helpless laughter. "His face! He expected me to maybe query the flour, but when *you* did, and when you then proceeded to be as rude to him as he was being to you! Standing there in your London toggery, sifting flour with your fingers in a manner born, and cursing as roundly as any fishwife!"

"Yes—and if any after-dinner chitchat ever comes to my ears concerning this episode, Marigold St. Aubrey, I'll put a ring through your nose!"

They spent an hour or so walking around the market, with Mally now and then stopping to speak with those she knew. Several of them asked after Maria, and she dutifully told them that her sister was staying with relatives. The bell of St. Crispin's rang out at midday and Mally stopped by the haberdashery stall to look at the church.

Annabel put back the braiding she had been examining.

"I married Daniel in that church at midday," murmured Mally softly.

"Well, the next wedding won't be a quiet country affair, will it?" said Annabel briskly. "Chris Carlyon's *do* will be fashionable and attended by *everyone*."

"It won't, you know. We're marrying here, not in London. And we shall not be inviting *everyone*."

"What a waste of a good wedding. If *I* were marrying him, I'd wheedle St. Paul's itself! No—Westminster Abbey!"

"With the Prince of Wales as best man?"

"*That* would be exquisite. But *you* must drag Chris to this backwood and sneak quite shiftily into the church. Are you afraid to marry him in an ostentatious blaze of showing-off, then?"

"No!"

"Don't looked outraged and full of jostling protests.

Oh, come now, Mally, since we've been here I've seen you time and time again deep in thought, staring at something or other. Beginning on our first evening here when you were gaping at the lily pond as if you expected a mermaid to appear at any moment. It's further back than Chris Carlyon that your thoughts are going still, isn't it?"

Mally knew that she was flushing, but could not help herself. "You are wrong," was all she could think of to say.

"No, I'm not," said Annabel softly, "and it's that one thing more than any other which makes Chris fair game still. I have not much time, Mally, but I shall use it, you may depend upon that."

"I know."

"I like you very much, Mally, but I *love* Chris."

"I know that too." Mally smiled. "And I have picked up that particular gauntlet."

"I had noticed. Still, all is not yet lost, not by a long chalk." Annabel picked up the braiding again and looked at it more closely. "What color would you say this is?"

"Puce."

"No, it isn't—puce is the color of my father's face when he's overindulged the maraschino. This is a darkish sort of purple, I fancy."

"It is still puce."

"Then I shall not buy it, for that word is one I do not like, and if I have to say that I am wearing puce braiding, it will be more than I could bear." She put it back, glancing at the woman behind the stall.

The woman was watching something over by the Three Feathers, and Annabel and Mally immediately turned to see what it was. Jasper Turney was deep in conversation with several other men, and they were gesticulating toward the church.

Annabel glanced around at the suddenly quiet market.

"There is an *atmosphere,* is there not, Mally? And the good Mr. Turney is in the very thick of it again."

Jasper turned then to shout back into the courtyard of the inn. "Brew?" he shouted clearly. "Brew? Get the others, that black feller's left his horse hidden in the churchyard. We reckon as he's gone to Towers! And hurry!"

Chapter 17

Mally gaped. "We must do something!"

"Such as? Mally, we are two mere women, we can hardly stop a mob such as the one now forming." Annabel looked around apprehensively. "We would be better advised getting ourselves well and truly away before anything happens."

"And leave them to hang that poor man? We can't!"

The men were moving away from the inn now, hurrying down the street toward the church.

"God Almighty, it isn't happening, it can't be—" Mally watched the faces of the people she had a moment before been speaking with. They wanted Abel dead, it was there in their eyes. Vindictive hatred.

There was shouting ahead by the church and the sound of a horse galloping up the street, the hooves echoing around the walls and windows of the houses.

The skewbald was swift, too swift for the outstretched hands of the nearest men as the negro flicked the reins from side to side, urging the animal faster. His leather jerkin flapped wildly and his hat flew off, revealing a tight mass of black curls, and Mally saw how wide and frightened his eyes were as he glanced behind at the men.

"Annabel, get back, he'll ride us down—" Mally pressed back behind the stall, still watching the approaching horse. "Annabel!"

But Annabel remained where she was, staring at the oncoming rider and the shouting men behind him, running back toward the market square.

"Annabel!" screamed Mally, beginning to step forward to snatch the other's arm.

But it was too late. The horse was upon them, dashing for the small gap between Annabel and the stall, and Mally was forced away again. Annabel was buffeted sideways and the horse swerved, throwing the negro heavily against the base of the stall, where he lay winded. Annabel sprawled in the mud by the goats' hurdles, and the frightened horse galloped on, its stirrups swinging and its reins trailing.

The crowd were stunned by the swiftness with which it had happened, and for a moment they stood where they were, the only sound being that of the horse. And then even that dwindled away to nothing. Jasper Turney's voice rang out. "We got 'im! We got 'im at last!"

His shout jerked the crowd from its immobility and they began to close in on the half-conscious man who still lay by the stall, his face contorted with pain. Mally pushed around the stall and stood by the Negro.

"No!" she cried. "Don't—"

A pistol shot rang out and she turned blindly in the direction of the sound. A landau had turned into the square, its roans sweating, and the Carlyon arms clearly visible on its lacquered doors. The door swung open and Richard Vallender climbed down, standing with one foot on the iron steps and a pistol balanced over his forearm.

"One more step, for anyone, and it will be their last, I promise you."

Annabel scrambled to her feet, wiping anxiously at the

dark stains and splatters of mud which covered her; but the anxious wiping was a nervous reaction, for she only made the marks worse.

Chris stepped down from the other side of the landau, tossing his spent pistol back inside. He paused to fluff the lace at his cuffs, glancing around the square almost casually.

Mally felt that she would burst into tears, but she crouched beside the injured man. "It's all right, Abel, it's all right now. Mr. Vallender is here—"

"Mas' Vallender?" Abel made as if he would get to his feet, but she pushed him gently back.

Chris came through the crowd toward her, and the people melted back before him. "Are you all right, Mally?"

"Yes. But Abel's hurt."

"You and Annabel go back to the landau, and quickly," he said quietly. "Richard's pistol has but one bullet and there are rather more than that gathered around us."

"But Abel—"

"He isn't heavy, I'll carry him." He smiled at her, touching her cheek gently. "Go on now and let us ease ourselves out of this den."

She straightened, catching Annabel's arm. "Leave the mud alone, Annabel, and come on—"

"But it's such a mess." Annabel's voice was curiously flat and toneless.

Mally glanced swiftly at her and then pulled her toward the landau. She turned as she heard the sound of a pony and trap. Dr. Towers was bringing the chestnut pony up to a smart pace and he halted in surprise as he came into the square and saw what was happening.

"Abel's hurt, Dr. Towers," explained Mally.

Chris picked up the injured man and carried him gently

to the landau. The doctor nodded at him. "Take him to the courthouse, and I will see him there."

Annabel climbed into the landau, still fussing about her ruined clothes, and Richard kept the pistol pointed over the crowd.

Abel reached out to him. "I had to come, Mas' Vallender."

Richard smiled quickly, putting his hand over the other's. "I know, Abel, I know."

The landau moved slowly around the square when Mally had climbed in, and the crowd remained stationary. Mally was shaking. What if the landau had not arrived at that moment? What might she and Annabel have witnessed? She glanced at Annabel again. The girl was staring at her soiled gloves. Chris put his arm around her worriedly.

"It's all right now, Annabel. Come on now."

She raised her head. "I just stood there, Chris, I stood like a lump of stone, and I caused the accident. It was my fault."

He squeezed her. "Don't be foolish."

"If he'd been killed, I would never have forgiven myself." Tears hung in her green eyes and she tried to blink them back, but they would not be denied. They meandered down her grimy cheeks.

Chris smiled fondly at her. "You're soft, Lady Annabel, do you know that?"

Abel lay across the other seat. He looked at Richard again. "Mas' Vallender, I came because—"

"All right, Abel!"

Mally's eyes went to Richard's face in surprise, and he patted the Negro's shoulder. "Tell me later."

"Yes, Mas'."

The landau slowed to enter the narrow gateway of the courthouse and inside the doctor's pony and trap had already arrived.

Annabel, Mally, and Chris climbed down, but Richard remained where he was as the doctor climbed in to examine Abel.

"Is he all right, Nathaniel?" he asked.

"Yes, I think so. In fact, I'm sure of it. He was badly winded, that's all."

"Then we'll go on up to the castle."

Mally leaned in. "But, Mr. Vallender, allow him a little time to recover."

"No, Mrs. St. Aubrey, I would rather do as I said. With all due thanks to you, of course."

She met his dark eyes. "As you wish, Mr. Vallender."

"I would hardly wish to foist my company upon your lady mother, would I?" He smiled. "You still intend coming?"

"Of course."

"I will see you then, whenever you wish to come."

She stepped back and the doctor climbed down, turning to look back at Richard. "I was coming up there anyway, Richard," he said. "Abel said that I was urgently needed. Damme, he wouldn't have dared come into Llanglyn for any other reason. You got my letter?"

"On the day I was leaving anyway."

"I thought you should know how things were faring back here."

Richard smiled. "You're a good friend, Nathaniel. Let's get on up there then. Chris, shall you come now or follow a little later?"

"Later, Richard. I'll use Mrs. Berrisford's barouche, which is already harnessed up." As if to underline his words, they heard the empty barouche halting outside on the road, unable to enter the courtyard because of the landau.

Richard's eyes went to Mally again. What was the expression she could see in them? Dislike? Anxiety? Mistrust? It could be anything. She watched the landau maneuver around the courtyard, conscious yet again that Richard Vallender did not want her at the castle. The pony and trap followed and soon the courtyard was empty, until the barouche's team nosed slowly beneath the gatehouse.

Mally nodded at the coachman. "Wait, if you please, Harris, for Sir Christopher wishes to go up to the castle a little later."

The coachman touched his hat, and Mally turned toward Chris and Annabel, noticing immediately that his arm was still around her shoulder in comfort. And Annabel was draining the last droplet of comfort she could from the prolonged moments. Mally's eyes flickered. "Still on the verge of the vapors, Annabel?"

"I feel quite distraught."

"That's one of my mother's favorite words. I had not realized you liked it too."

Chris raised his eyebrow. "Let's get inside, shall we?"

"Oh." Mally closed her eyes briefly. "I've left Mother's shopping in the market."

"Judging by the motley selection of persons gathered there today, that's the last you'll see of the shopping. Basket and all."

They crossed toward the wood steps and climbed to the gallery where Pattie waited anxiously.

"Oh, Lady Annabel, whatever's been happening?"

"More Llanglyn merry-making," said Annabel flatly, allowing Pattie to usher her away from Chris and into the great hall.

Chris caught Mally back gently. "What's going on here, Mally?"

"The people think Mr. Vallender's Abel killed Mrs. Harmon."

"And did he? In your opinion?"

She considered. "No. I believe Dr. Towers when he says Abel did not."

"It's strange, but Richard was anxious to get back here sooner. It was almost as if he sensed things were wrong."

"Then why didn't he? Surely he could have returned had he really wished to."

"I begin to think you are not impressed by Richard, Mally."

"Oh, I'm impressed. Most impressed."

Chris prudently left the matter, beginning to walk on, but she remained at the top of the steps. "Chris, why *didn't* he come back then?"

"He couldn't. He'd sold his horse and was depending upon me to bring him home."

"He sold that horse? But why?"

Chris came back to her. "To pay Dr. Stiller. I know that to be so, for the last thing we did before leaving London was to call at Stiller's house."

"Is Mr. Vallender ill then?"

"If he is, then he is keeping the fact to himself. He said nothing of Stiller and I did not ask him." He smiled, slipping his arms around her waist. "I missed you."

She kissed him, holding him tightly. But she felt guilty as she did so, for it was not of him that she was thinking at that moment. It was Richard Vallender's visit to Dr. Stiller. And who it was up at Castell Melyn who required Dr. Towers so urgently—urgently enough for Abel to risk his life coming into Llanglyn? Was it Maria. Was she up at Castell Melyn, and was she ill?

Chris closed the door of Mally's room quietly and she turned quickly from staring up at Castell Melyn.

"Your mother is working up to a fine pitch over this impending tea party. I came up here to escape."

"Couldn't Annabel keep you in her clutches any longer then?"

He paused. "She *is* upset, Mally, and still shakes all over."

"I'll warrant she does! Quivering like a doe each time you touch her, leaning winsomely against your manly shoulder and turning those great cow-eyes adoringly toward you all the time! *I* came up here to escape as well!"

He smiled. "I'll warrant she's making all the headway she can, which flatters me quite considerably. But that doesn't mean she is faking how she feels about what happened in Llanglyn earlier."

"Headway can only be made under favorable conditions," said Mally shortly, biting her lip and looking away.

"That wasn't called for. And I would be a poor friend to her if I snubbed her over such a thing, wouldn't I? Annabel's all right and I like her."

"So I noticed."

"I am her friend, not her lover. Come on now, Mally, stop this—" He put his hand to the nape of her neck and wound his fingers gently in her warm hair. "You're in a miff with me, aren't you? Mm?"

She looked at him immediately. "With you? No. With myself."

"I'll pass over such a cryptic, entirely female remark." He pulled her nearer and kissed her.

She closed her eyes and moved to hold him tightly. She was angry, angry and confused. Each tiny inch Annabel strove to creep nearer to him could have been halted. *I could have smacked her down in no uncertain way. But I did nothing, nothing at all—*

He drew his finger over her lips, softly and slowly. "You're in a stew over your sister still?"

She seized the straw. "There's been no word."

"No news is good news, so they say."

"Just a scribbled note would be all she need do."

"An escape to Richard's ghost-ridden pile of stone will do you good. It will take your mind from Miss Maria Berrisford's misdemeanors for a while. Now that your mother has realized that Annabel knows about your sister, she has done nothing but rattle about it. And about the tea party. And about Mrs. Clevely. And about the gossips of Llanglyn. And about poor Richard, who is blacker than black in her eyes. She never stops. I think your father *threw* himself from that damned horse, *he* needed an escape as well."

She smiled. "Mother cannot help it."

"Anyone can help chattering quite so much. Anyway, I shall go up to Castell Melyn now, but I shall come back for you and Annabel tonight."

"Tonight?"

"Why not?"

"Mother—"

"Damn Mother. You and Annabel need rescuing, and in true white-knight fashion, I am doing my chivalrous act. Tonight."

She nodded, kissing him for a last time. The afternoon sun was thin and watery as she looked up at Castell Melyn again. Tonight she would be there, and perhaps at long last she might begin to find some of the answers to the various puzzles and mysteries which surrounded Maria.

Chapter 18

It was raining as the landau moved slowly up the lane, and the window was awash, distorting the shadowy trees outside. The wind had strengthened, moaning through the woods, sending stray dead leaves to cling to the glass as Mally looked out into the night. They slid slowly down until the wind caught them again, spinning them away into the wild darkness.

Annabel shivered. "Had I begged for an *atmosphere*, I could not have hoped for better."

Chris tucked the traveling rug around her knees again. "Imagination is a wondrous thing."

"You are jealous because you have none. Oh, I wonder if the ghosts sense my approach."

Mally groaned. "Yes, they are at this very moment hurrying out through the back door, their chains rattling in terror."

"Castles don't have back doors, they have posterns. Nothing you two say will deflate me, I am *determined* to be in a state of goose-pimpled anticipation for the whole of my stay."

"Will your constitution withstand such an onslaught?" Chris grinned at her.

"I have the constitution of an ox."

Mally raised an eyebrow. "You said it."

"To save you."

"You didn't seem to have much resistance to anything out of the ordinary earlier today, wilting here and there like some fading blossom." Mally tugged some of the traveling rug back.

"I know. I'm ashamed of myself, actually."

"So you should be. Constitution of an ox indeed." Mally gave a final tug and recovered her portion of the rug. She felt Chris glance at her and steadfastly avoided his eyes.

Annabel looked out at the wind-lashed woods. "This is like some nightmare land, isn't it? All howling wind, heavy rain, and whispering trees. Not for anyone of an even *vaguely* nervous disposition."

"Which must include your good self for a start," said Mally. "But then, you must be the only person in the land who actually looks forward to being scared witless. Oh, just look at how the wind is bending those trees over there, the gale is getting stronger with each minute. I'll warrant Dr. Towers is glad he returned to Llanglyn when he did."

Chris nodded. "He set up a spanking pace down the hill, I can tell you. We could see the storm approaching across the northern mountains, watching the cloud and rain swallow each one in turn. The baron who built that castle certainly knew a vantage point when he saw it, for there's nothing for miles which cannot be seen and overlooked from up there."

"Who is ill up there?" asked Mally casually.

"A groom. Richard and Towers were worried."

"What's wrong with him?"

"Couldn't say. When I asked, Richard said that they'd taken the advice of the best doctor in the land—"

"Stiller?"

"Perhaps. He is acknowledged one of the best."

Annabel looked surprise. "Dr. Stiller for a mere *groom?* How very eccentric."

The landau slowed to a halt and immediately the rushing and hissing of the trees was louder and more menacing. Lanterns swayed on the walls of the lodge, casting moving light and dark over the lane and making the raindrops on the windows glisten like diamonds. The lodgekeeper came out, his cloak flapping, and a heavy metallic creaking cut into the night, making the landau's team start nervously.

"What's that?" said Annabel immediately.

"The portcullis," said Chris. "Even the lodge has a portcullis and a drawbridge. The gateway to Castell Melyn is one of the most extravagant I've come across and I've come across a fair number."

"More extravagant than Lord Hayldon's Eastern-palace affair?" asked Annabel.

"Hayldon would be put to shame."

The landau lurched forward again, echoing hollowly beneath the narrow arched gateway with its squat towers. Torches flared on the walls, their flames tipping and smoking in the storm, and then the wheels were rolling over wood.

"The drawbridge," said Chris before Annabel could speak. "There is a false moat and a drawbridge which is lowered to let anyone in. I tell you, if that drawbridge was raised, then no one could get in or out of the park, for every inch of the castle's land is well and truly enclosed. With a wall."

"Then there is no going back, is there?" Annabel turned up the rich fur collar of her pelisse and wriggled further back in the seat.

"How very fatal that sounds," said Mally, glancing from the window at the wide park. There were few trees now, only the park stretching up toward the castle. The unfettered wind buffeted across the mountainside and the landau shook with each gust. She could see the castle against the sky; at least, she could see that single light in the southwest tower—

Mally was trembling as the landau moved even nearer, and with each yard covered she could make out more of the fortress. The towers were just visible now, standing square and strong, and the curtain wall plunging down to the rock on which it was built. As the landau swung around the drive, the lights on the drawbridge glittered in the rippled water of the moat, and smoke from the chimneys of the newly restored living apartments was caught and spun down over the water, threading and tearing like cobwebs. It drifted into the landau, sharp and acrid, and once more the rain splattered the windows as the landau turned against the wind.

Chris wiped the moisture from the glass. "Annabel, you have your atmosphere—with a vengeance, eh?"

"Yes. It is perfect. Absolutely perfect."

The teams drew the carriage over the drawbridge and the wind was suddenly closed off by the great barbican. The uneven old stones made the carriage sway and jolt, and the team's hooves sent sparks flashing from the paving.

Servants ran from a doorway as the landau halted, and the flambeaux they carried burned steadily in the almost windless courtyard. The door was opened and the sound of the rain was immediately louder, but the great walls and towers shielded the courtyard from the worst of the storm. Chris helped Mally and Annabel down and an old man in a powdered wig and rust-colored coat and breeches bowed politely, indicating a doorway with the sweep of his hand. His face was wizened and dark, and his brown button eyes were sharp and bright.

"Mesdames. Milord."

Mally grinned at Annabel. "You've been demoted."

"Blue blood will out," retorted Annabel as they stepped thankfully into the warmth of the converted buttery where the cask racks now held a collection of colored glass and porcelain. A sole remaining butt stood in one corner, and on it a large polished copper bowl containing tumbling sprays of Michaelmas daisies and chrysanthemums, with here and there the bright red berries of the rowans which lined the lower half of the drive. Annabel surveyed the arrangement in surprise. "Berries in the house! How very novel, don't you think so, Chris?"

"An American notion, I believe. There's an arrangement of brambles, old man's beard, and holly in the solar. Takes getting used to, but I confess I like it."

There was a smell of cinnamon and wine in the buttery, as if all the old spices had seeped into the walls over the centuries. The stone floor was scrubbed clean and some Eastern rugs lay here and there, bright designs of color and tone to soften the stark whitewash of the walls. Mally looked around.

"It's so different. The last time I was here, this was all cobwebs, dirty old casks, and dust. The door was half off its hinges and creaked most horribly with each tiny draft." She shivered.

Daniel, you let me out of here this instant! Do you hear me? Please, I'm frightened!

The old man took their cloaks and mantles, and then bowed. Without a smile he indicated that they should follow him once more. Mally glanced at Annabel, who looked as if she could have a fit of the giggles at the strange, silent little man. They left the smell of cinnamon behind as they walked further into the castle, passing a grandfather clock which ticked slowly and loudly, its walnut cabinet soft and rich in the lamp light. Beside it was a portrait of a woman in a rather old-fashioned pink gown. Her name was on the frame. Gillian Vallender—1806. Mally paused, looking up at Richard Vallender's wife, at the wistful, lost smile of the woman he had never truly loved. The sadness was there in the sweet face. Perhaps Gillian had not been as unaware as he had thought—

They went up some winding, worn stone steps where the bare walls were hung with swords and daggers. The air was musty, and as they passed the newly glazed slit windows they could hear the storm raging.

Richard Vallender stood by the fireplace in the solar, and he smiled at them. "The storm did not deter you then?" His hand was warm as he greeted Mally. "Welcome to Castell Melyn."

Annabel looked around. "What a very pleasing room, Mr. Vallender."

"The only pleasing room in the place, apart from the bedrooms. The great hall is just that—great! And drafty, and gloomy, and sadly lacking its attendant forest of retainers, serfs, boarhounds, minstrels, and so on. Does the new Castell Melyn meet with *your* approval, Mrs. St. Aubrey?"

She allowed her gaze to wander slowly around. The large windows overlooking the courtyard were concealed behind heavy ruby-red curtains, and the walls had been plastered and whitewashed. The wooden floor was stained dark brown, and before the fire a thick carpet patterned in wine and cream was lit by the huge, licking flames in the ancient fireplace. The furniture was richly upholstered in pale green, and arrangements of flowers and berries stood on the many tables, their highly polished copper bowls gleaming in the half-light. High above hung an old, iron-rimmed candleholder, throwing up a ring of brightness to the rafters in the gloom of the ceiling. There was a painting of a large white house above the fireplace, and many smaller paintings and portraits hung on the walls. At the far end, one large tapestry covered the entire wall, a beautiful scene of medieval lords and ladies, hawks and dogs moving across a landscape of strange trees and plants.

She looked at Richard again. "It's very, very beautiful, Mr. Vallender, far more than pleasing."

He smiled. "That is praise indeed. Louis, *ypocras, s'il vous plaît.*"

The butler bowed. *"Oui, monsieur."*

When he had gone, Annabel sat down in the chair closest to the fire. "Is your Louis a Frenchman then?"

"No. A Creole. From New Orleans."

"How very superior, quite a talking point in many a drawing room. I envy you."

"I wouldn't know, Lady Annabel. Please sit down, Mrs. St. Aubrey—would it be presuming upon our friendship at all if I begged permission to call you Mally? Daniel was a grand fellow, but his name was ever a mouthful."

She smiled, allowing him to lead her to a chair. "Please call me Mally. But then I must call you Richard, must I not?"

"That would be fair, yes." He smiled again as she looked up at him. His eyes were so very dark, that try as she could she could not see into them.

Louis returned with a tray of warmed glasses and a jug of spiced wine. The *ypocras* was perfect, just the needed warmth for the cold night, and Annabel sipped hers appreciatively. Her face shone with the glow of the fire as she turned to Richard.

"Have you seen Lady Jacquetta, Mr. Vallender? Richard."

"Not a whisker."

"No rattlings, moanings, or unearthly shrieks?"

He shook his head, smiling. "Not one, I fear."

"Oh, dear, she will have to do better than this. This is

my great sallying forth into the realms of the afterworld, and the very least she could do is send an icy chill over the room or something."

As she finished speaking the door flew open, banging loudly against a chair. The cold air from the steps swept over the room, fluttering the candles and dragging a cloud of smoke from the fire. Annabel's eyes were huge and she swallowed the last of the wine in one mouthful. Mally shuddered, for the timing had been uncanny. Chris smothered a laugh.

The butler's wrinkled face was expressionless. *"C'est la porte extérieur, monsieur, pardonnez moi."*

Richard grinned. *"Cą ne fait rien, Louis. Merci."*

"Monsieur."

When the door had closed again, the fire stopped smoking and the candles settled back to their steady burning. Annabel breathed out loudly. "I'd swear that man knew the door would blow open! Does he understand English, Mr.—Richard?"

"Oh, perfectly. But he persists in speaking French and I'm afraid it's easier to do things his way than it is to try to change him."

Chris was still laughing at Annabel's pale face. "So, it was no chain-rattling ghost, just a medieval door with a medieval latch!"

"Stop laughing, Chris. You have to admit it was *most* alarming, coming just when I had spoken. Almost"—she looked sharply at Richard—"almost as expertly timed as that dreadful goddess with staring eyes."

He put his hand to his heart. "Now would *I* be guilty of such a heartless joke?"

"Yes. You and Chris together would be perfectly capable of dreaming up countless such coincidences to keep me squeaking. What have you set up in this place, eh? Look me in the eye and say you are innocent!"

Richard leaned closer, looking straight at her. "I am innocent, my sweet lady. Absolutely and completely."

Mally watched him. He was outwardly relaxed, smiling, and being a perfect host. Yet there was still a slight tension in him whenever he looked toward Mally, something reserved, although he spoke charmingly and smiled a great deal. No matter how he tried, he could not completely conceal the unease Mally's presence caused him, and she sensed it strongly.

"Tell me, Richard," she said, "how is poor Abel now?"

"Recovered. And bruised. But Nathaniel assures me no damage has been done."

"And the groom? I trust there is good news there too."

He stared at her. "Groom?"

"Why yes, the man Dr. Towers was coming to see so urgently anyway today."

"Ah. He is not well, I fear."

"What's wrong with him?" asked Annabel curiously, wondering again about the great Dr. Stiller being approached for a servant.

Richard poured himself another glass of *ypocras*. Mally knew that he was giving himself time, for he took a long time over such a simple task. "He—er, had an experience which affected his mind. No, Lady Annabel, not a ghostly experience, a very flesh-and-blood one. He was set upon when returning from Hereford one night, and was left for dead. He was found and had a letter addressed to me here at the castle and so they brought him back. Dr. Towers attended him, and we thought at first that he was unconscious only as anyone would be after such an assault, but then it became apparent that it was something more. He has lain there now for some weeks, quite unconscious and yet very much alive."

Annabel held her glass out to him. "Is that why you have been visiting Dr. Stiller?"

Richard glanced accusingly at Chris, who looked

uncomfortably guilty. "Yes, Lady Annabel, that is why I sought Stiller's advice."

"Which is? Oh, forgive my morbid persistence, Richard, but I'm very interested," said Annabel, clinging to the subject like a limpet.

"He says that in his experience such disorders of the mind can only ever be overcome by a repetition of the experience which brought it about in the first place. In other words, someone has to set about him, or he has to see someone else being set about. That might squeeze the trigger in his head, or whatever it is in his head which is keeping him in such a state."

Annabel stared. "Someone must beat the poor man all over again? I would imagine that would have sent him further away from this world, not brought him back again."

He smiled faintly. "That, Lady Annabel, is exactly how I feel."

"So, you intend doing nothing?" asked Chris.

"For the moment. I feel quite helpless."

"And does his condition allow you such time to consider?" asked Annabel.

"To look at him, one would imagine that time is endless." Richard drained his glass. Mally caught the heartfelt tone in his voice; it was not of the groom's illness that he spoke—

Annabel put her glass down. "Well, I am ready."

"For what?" asked Mally.

"The bugaboos and ghosties, of course."

"Tonight?" said Chris in surprise.

"Why yes. What better time? The wind is howling and the storm raging. I want to ghost-hunt right now."

Chris smiled. "Two glasses of *ypocras* and you'll take on the entire demon kingdom. All right, I'm game. Come on Mally, Richard—we'll let Lady Fearless here take the lead."

Mally stood, looking at Richard. "Shall we start with the southwest tower?"

His eyes flickered. "Why there?"

"It interests me—I've seen the light burning there so long."

"That is because the groom is there, Mally," he said softly. "I don't think we should do our hunting there now, do you?"

He held her gaze for a moment and she nodded at last. "Perhaps not."

Chapter 19

The great hall was dark and hollow. The solitary candle Chris held made small inroads on the gloom which stretched on all echoing sides, and Mally's heart was thundering. Suddenly it seemed that Annabel's ghosts were not so laughable and distant after all. The wind's sad wailing pressed all around the outside of the building which stood alone on the northern side of the courtyard, and dry leaves scuttered in through the door before Richard closed it behind them.

"Well, and here you have my great hall." *Hall—hall—hall—* His voice kept swinging back at them from the darkness.

Chris's voice held humor. "I can imagine that your good self in solitary splendor in this cavern *would* be a little lost."

"Aye, my friend, like a pimple on an elephant."

High above something fluttered in the rafters and Annabel melted against Chris, gazing up to try to make out what it was. Mally's heart would not cease its thundering, and she wished herself back in the gentle solar—

"A barn owl," said Richard. "I doubt that he has to

leave this place at any time, there are more than enough rats to keep him too fat to fly."

"Rats?" Annabel sought Chris's hand. "In here?"

"Yes." Mally could hear the mirth in Richard's voice.

"Well, why do you not keep some beast to control them?" Annabel's fingers twined determinedly around Chris's.

"The Pied Piper was otherwise engaged." Richard took a long breath. "Besides, I don't think I shall be requiring this mausoleum for a long, long time."

Chris was surprised. "But, Richard, I have seen this place in the daylight. It's very splendid still and would make the ballroom to end all ballrooms."

"Maybe, but such funds as I had were more than stretched to cover the rest of the castle. Mally here will tell you it was a ruin, more or less. Some rooms were still intact, but that is all that can be said."

"Some parts were still too intact," she murmured, remembering.

Richard looked at her. "You let the past prey on you, Mally," he said softly.

She walked further on into the hall, her footsteps echoing. The darkness seemed to press in, and the fluttering of the barn owl was renewed. She hesitated. "Is there anything leading from his hall? I don't remember."
Remember—remember—remember— She spoke rather louder than she had intended and her voice slid from corner to corner, swooping back at her from all sides.

"The kitchens," said Richard. "Over there."

Chris removed his hand from Annabel's fingers. "I'll show you." He gave Annabel the candle and came closer to Mally, slipping his arm around her waist. "This way."

Annabel's voice followed them. "Lady Jacquetta wouldn't be seen *dead* in the kitchens!" Then she laughed at her own joke.

The light from that solitary candle was so faint now

that Mally and Chris could hardly see, and he turned to ask Annabel to bring it nearer. But at that moment the candle went out.

Mally halted as the velvety completeness of the darkness made her completely blind. "Annabel?"

"Richard," said Chris, "open the door—"

"I'll bring another light."

The door opened and closed, sounding loud and final. The closing of the door brought the past creeping back to touch Mally with cold fingers. The darkness locked her in, and the wind howled outside just as it had all those years ago in this very castle—

You let me out of here this instant! Do you hear me! Daniel! Please!

"Daniel?" The word slipped out, and she caught Chris's hand.

Then Richard was there again with a light and the past was driven back. But the mistake had been made. She turned to Chris. The look in his eyes told her how much of a gap had suddenly appeared between them. He took his hand away from her. "My name is Chris," he said flatly. "Once again you appear to have forgotten." *Forgotten—forgotten—forgotten—* The echo took his voice.

"It was the past—" she began, her voice shaking.

"It is now the present for most of us." His eyes were cold.

Richard held the new candle to the dead wick and after a moment there was more light. The barn owl's white heart-shaped face peered down at them from high above. It screeched loudly, the screech seeming to go on forever as the deadly echo seized upon it.

Annabel glanced from Mally to Chris. "I didn't mean—"

Mally rounded on her. "You blew the candle out, didn't you?"

"It was only fun—"

"*Fun!* Oh, damn you, damn you to hell!" *Hell—hell—hell—*

"Mally—" Annabel looked unhappy. "Forgive me, I meant only to get my own back on Chris for that business with the statue."

Chris held his hand out to Annabel. "Come on then, let's continue our search."

Mally stood miserably where she was, watching how eagerly Annabel reached out to him. They walked on toward the door at the far end where the kitchens were at the base of the northern tower.

Richard looked at her. "You look as if you've seen Annabel's ghost," he said softly.

"There *was* a ghost," she said with a small laugh, "and it was very real. Just for a moment."

He took her hand. "Shall we follow? If we do not, the fair Annabel may make more ground up than even she dreams of."

"Perhaps."

He held the candle and studied her face, his dark eyes seeming fathomless. "Chris wants you, Annabel wants Chris. But you, Mally, what do you want?"

"I don't know what you mean." She began to walk on.

He held her. "I mean that for a love match, you and Chris seem to have precious little understanding."

"That's nonsense," she said, smiling brightly. The trembling was passing; but the swiftness of Chris's coldness was numbing—

"Is it? Then forgive me." He led her on toward the kitchens, where the other candle's light was bobbing and shaking, and where Annabel's laughter was at odds with the gloom in the hall.

"Not a shriek, not a single mournful wail!" Annabel sat down on the green velvet sofa in the solar and accepted the glass Richard held out to her. "How very frustrating."

"The ghosts probably have been caught unawares by the suddenness of your arrival, Annabel." Richard laughed. "Tomorrow I am certain they will put on their party piece for you."

"After such excellent Creole cooking and such magnificent wine, Richard, I will forgive them. You are an excellent host." She smiled at him. "I like your castle, Richard Vallender, but you simply must do up that hall and make it into a ballroom. The gallery at the end is perfect for an orchestra—which is what the minstrels were, weren't they?"

"They were. Perhaps, one day—"

"And if we could winkle out the good Lady Jacquetta and persuade her to put on a performance, you'd have every fashionable name in England clamoring to cross the Welsh border, beating your door for an invitation!"

"God forbid." Richard laughed and sat down.

"But first of all we must find the place where she was walled up."

"Why?" asked Chris, taking a seat next to her. He was still cool toward Mally, who after a few attempts at melting him had now resigned herself to being virtually ignored. And this time, it was so very unfair—

Annabel sniffed her glass of Madeira. "Because, as every good ghost-hunter knows, that would be the place she is chained to. Spiritually now, of course."

"Poppycock." Chris laughed.

"It isn't! Anyway, I have here in my reticule a vastly interesting book on the subject of Castell Melyn and Lady Jacquetta. I wheedled at my father to prevail upon his good friend, the Constable of the Tower of London. They belong to the same club, don't you know." Her voice dropped into a perfect, wheezy imitation of her father. "And the good Constable nosed this out." She put the book on the table before them. It was small, covered with well-worn black leather, with a tiny metal clasp.

"What does it say?" asked Richard, picking it up and flicking idly through the ancient pages.

"I won't go into the same gruesome detail as the book. Lady Jacquetta and her husband Sir Francis belong to the time of the Wars of the Roses. She was being unfaithful to him with a certain Sir Piers Grasville, who together with Francis supported Richard III. Jacquetta's misdemeanors were discovered, Sir Piers escaped, Sir Francis took umbrage in a very determined way, walling his wife up and turning coat to support the invading Henry Tudor. So, if it had not been for my ghostly lady, one must assume that Henry Tudor would not have found his invasion through Wales quite such a simple matter. And there you have the tale—in a nutshell. Is it not entertaining?"

Chris nodded and raised his glass to her. "Most definitely."

Annabel leaned forward, her eyes huge in the firelight. "Perhaps he could hear her after he'd had her walled up—screaming, begging, tearing her bloodied fingers on the very walls—"

Richard glanced quickly at Mally's pale face. "I think that's enough of Lady Jacquetta's fate, don't you think?"

"And I was just warming to my subject," Annabel protested.

"Mally isn't, and with good reason, I fancy," said Richard.

"I'd forgotten." Annabel looked penitent. "Mally, I didn't think—"

"It's all right, Annabel, why should you remember something like that?" Mally did not glance at Chris at all. *He* should have remembered, though—

"Was it very frightening?" went on Annabel persistently.

"Yes." Mally didn't want to talk about it anymore. "Richard, what house is that in the painting?"

Richard turned toward the fireplace. "Le Bosquet Bas—my late wife's plantation outside New Orleans."

"It's very beautiful."

"You should not go by appearances, Mally." He glanced at her, smiling.

"Wasn't it beautiful then?"

"A damned prison. For Gillian anyway." He finished his drink and picked up the decanter. "Now, to more pleasing subjects. A game of faro? Backgammon? *Vingt-et-un?*"

Annabel clapped her hands. "Backgammon. I have yet to beat Chris, and so tonight I shall do my utmost."

It was done so swiftly that Mally was almost breathless. Annabel had seized upon the one game which required only two players, and she had pinned Chris to partner her— Mally said nothing, made no move to suggest another game, and she was aware of Chris glancing at her. Richard brought the backgammon board and pieces and drew a small table before the sofa.

He smiled blandly at Chris and Annabel. "We will leave you to it then. Come, Mally, I have something to show you."

Still not looking at Chris, she stood and took the hand Richard held out to her. They walked from the solar, leaving the other two suddenly rather quiet.

Outside on the steps, Richard paused, turning to look up at her where she stood on the landing. "You should make up your mind, you know, Mally—make it up once and for all and stick to your decision."

"What do you mean?"

"Your attitude to your engagement. I have observed you, you are in what I believe is termed a dither. One moment you seem to want Chris, and the next—"

"I think you said you had something to show me."

"I have. Don't look so frostily at me."

"I just don't want to discuss my affairs with you."

"Fair enough." He led her on down the cold stairs.

Outside in the courtyard it was still raining and they could plainly hear the wind moaning and wailing around the battlements. Mally glanced up at the south tower. The light burned on.

Chapter 20

The cobbles were slippery, shining with the reflections of torches and lamps as Mally hurried across behind Richard. A torch flared and crackled by the low arched door at the foot of the Norman keep, and Richard drew her into the lee of the keep as he reached up to lift a rusty key from a hook by the door.

Mally laughed. "Surely you aren't taking me into the dungeon?"

"That's exactly where I'm taking you."

Her smile faded. "I have had enough of such things tonight—"

He pushed the key into the lock. "There's something I think you'd like to see in there. Oh, don't begin to think of miserable things from the past again—" He caught her hand as the door opened. "Think of some more pleasant times for a change."

The rain pattered in on the dry, worn steps inside, and as Richard lifted the torch down from its bracket, the light leaped down the chilly stairway leading to the castle's single, deep dungeon. The air was unbelievably cold and the dampness was clinging, seeping into everything. Richard handed her the torch and took off his coat, wrapping it around her shoulders. There was a faint drift of sandalwood clinging to it.

He looked at her as he took the torch again. "You aren't afraid, are you?"

"No."

She followed him on down, glancing at the monstrous shadows cast by the torch, shadows which seemed to coil and recoil as if about to pounce. The stone slabs at the foot of the steps were wet and the walls ran with moisture as they walked to the end of the low passage.

The door of the dungeon was open and the light seemed to swamp the tiny square room as Richard stepped inside. She could hear the spluttering and hissing of the flame as she stood looking around.

"This at least hasn't changed," she said.

"Ah, so you remember it."

"Of course—one of the worst dares we could think of was to come down here alone and count to one hundred."

"But you don't remember everything, do you?"

"Why do you say that?"

"Here."

He went to a far corner where the wall was surprisingly dry, and raised the torch closer to the wall. She stared at the two words carved there in rough, childish scrawl. *Daniel. Mally.* And a heart.

Oh, go on, Mally, no one's going to know we've written here!

But it's not our castle, Daniel, not really.

Yes it is, but we've got to let it know. We'll have a castle one day, Mally, all to ourselves—

She turned away. "I'd forgotten," she whispered. "It was a June day, the hottest that summer. Oh, we did get into trouble when we got back, because we'd slipped away from Maria and she'd been left alone all day—" She looked at him suddenly, she should ask him about Maria. Now was the right time surely—

He pushed the torch into an ancient bracket on the wall nearby. "I'll warrant Maria didn't appreciate that very much."

She couldn't say it, she couldn't accuse him— "She didn't, she told tales on me for a month after that and I hated her so much I cut her hair when she was asleep. And that got me into boiling oil for another month."

"I can't believe you'd be so willful, Mally. Maria, yes. But not you."

"I had my less lovable moments."

"Mally, there's nothing I can say about Maria, you know. Don't look so surprised, it was written all over your face that you wanted to ask me again."

"I'm sorry I was so obvious."

He smiled, leaning back against the wall. The frill at the front of his white shirt was intricate and costly, and the white fabric bright even in the dim light of the torch. "As you say, you have your moments."

"And what does that mean?"

"Well, not so very many minutes ago you most firmly said you didn't wish to discuss your affairs with me, so perhaps I should not say—"

"This is most unfair. You cannot make cryptic remarks and then shy away from explanation."

He smiled. "Very well. You are obvious—to me— when you let Annabel cleave even closer to Chris."

"I don't—"

"Oh, yes you do. You could give her elbow a nudge which would have her arm in a sling for a year, but you don't even tap her on the shoulder and wag your disapproving finger. Tonight, for instance. The backgammon."

She flushed. "I was in a miff with Chris."

"That wasn't why. But it *is* another thing. You are content to let him be in a miff with you, aren't you?"

"Richard, I don't think it's right to go on talking like this, it isn't fair—"

"Who to? Chris?"

She said nothing.

"Mally, what you're doing now is unfair to Chris. You'll never give completely to him. Because there's tenderness, but no deep understanding. You don't love him as much as you loved Daniel."

She turned to leave, but he caught her hand and pulled her back. "Let me go, Richard, please!"

"No, for you'll rush off in a miff with me too." He smiled. "I have already told you that I know what I'm talking about. Marriage with a second-best is senseless, and in your case very wrong. I know what I'm talking about, for I've been here before you, Mally, and everything I see you doing now I once did myself. I recognize all the signs."

"It could—which heaven forbid, of course—be that you are wrong for once."

"I'm not. You are a woman of the world, Mally, and you *know* your love for Chris is somewhat less than Chris's for you. What happens then when you meet a man who sets you by your ears, whose very glance melts you? As Daniel's glance melted you, but Chris's never will. Answer me that."

"Are these the same persuasive arguments you used when my sister met Andrew York?"

He raised his eyebrows. "Maria needed no telling, Mally. *She* could see for herself that the dreadful Thomas was too dreadful for contemplation. She wanted Andrew and he wanted her, and that was the end of it."

"And I need telling, is that what you mean?"

"In a way. You too can see for yourself the mistake you're making, but you're like spindrift, carried along by the force of outside influences and not stopping once and for all to say exactly what you really feel."

"I can't hurt him."

"It's getting to the point where he's hurting you—in self-defense."

"I don't know that I like being understood so completely when I hardly know you."

He smiled. "I said—I have been there before you. And I feel that I know you because I know Maria so well."

"How well?" she breathed.

"As an intended member of my family. Andrew was my wife's cousin."

She stared at him. She wanted to believe him, and yet she could not. Maria was here, in this castle, she was sure of it, and that certainty mounted with each passing moment. Maria was somewhere close by. In that south tower perhaps?

He put his hand to her face suddenly. "You look so confused and uncertain, and you should not be. It is born of your engagement to Chris, and will remain as long as that ring is on your finger."

"You do not care that you suggest I wreck Chris's happiness?"

"I do nothing I do not think Chris is already beginning to realize for himself. But he will cling to you, I feel, because he's always loved and wanted you. What man would not want you?"

Her face felt hot. "We'd better go back—"

"Why?" He took her hand and pulled her closer. "Because you fear being closed in?"

"I'm not afraid of that now."

"No, because you're with me." His mouth was soft as he kissed her, and then he drew back. "Give Chris his ring back, Mally, You're not for him."

She couldn't speak, staring at him. Then she turned and hurried from the dungeon and up into the rain-beaten night.

Someone was standing in the courtyard calling Richard. It was Abel, the rain making his black skin shine as he held his leather jerkin over his head against the storm.

"Mas' Vallender! Mas' Vallender!" He turned as he heard Mally. "You know where Mas' Vallender is, Miss Maria?"

She halted as she heard her sister's name on his lips. Her heart was thundering, both from what had happened in the dungeon and now from this new shock. "Yes, Abel, he's in the dungeon."

Abel seemed uncertain, coming closer and peering at her through the darkness. "Thank you, Miss M———" His mouth snapped shut as he realized his mistake, and his eyes were large suddenly. He ran past her and through the doorway at the foot of the keep.

Mally stood in the rain, holding Richard's coat around her shoulders. Maria *was* here, she had been right. She stared at the black doorway where the door swung in the draft of cold air. The gale moaned around the castle and the rain lashed over the courtyard, splashing into the ever-increasing puddles which gathered in each dip and crevice. Richard had lied. After all that, he had still lied. She looked up at the tower where the light still burned.

Richard followed Abel up from the dungeon and he stopped as he saw her. They stared at each other for a moment, and then he nodded at Abel.

"Get my horse and I'll see what's been going on down there."

"The tree down, Mas' Vallender. Maybe more go down."

"Get the horse."

Abel nodded, glancing worriedly from Richard to Mally, and then he looked at Richard again. "I'm sorry, Mas' Vallender—"

"That's all right, Abel. Now get on with it."

The Negro's steps splashed away across the courtyard, and Richard turned to Mally. "Mally?"

She shook her head, and turned to run toward the door leading to the solar. She didn't know what to do, but for the moment she wanted to be away from Richard Vallender at all costs. As she pushed the door open and went in from the rain, she almost screamed, for Louis was standing there.

"*Madame?*" He bowed politely.

She glanced back out in the rain, but Richard had gone. Louis stood silently, watching her.

"Louis, *où est ma chambre, s'il vous plaît?*" It sounded so horribly lame, but it was all she could think of, and the thought of a room where she could be alone to think was reassuring.

"*Madame.*" He bowed again, indicating that she should follow him. With one final look at the stormy night, she hurried after him.

Chapter 21

The maid bobbed an awkward curtsey, wiping her nervous hands on her crumpled apron.

"*Mishur* Louis said as I was to attend you, ma'am." Her eyes were frightened and she straightened her mobcap anxiously, pushing a black plait neatly beneath it.

"That would be kind of you— What is your name?"

"Gwynneth, ma'am."

"Gwynneth. Are you from Llanglyn?"

"No, ma'am, from over the mountains at Crickhowell."

Mally took Richard's damp coat from her shoulders and set it carefully over a chair. A fireplace had been built recently, its yellow stone standing out from the worn, ancient stones of the rest of the room. Some pretty tapestries hung on one wall, and a gold-framed painting of a woman with some hunting dogs. The fourposter bed was immense, dominating the room, and its beautiful dull blue curtains found an echo in the sapphire-colored carpet which almost fitted from wall to wall it was made so exactly to the size of the room. A narrow slit window high on one wall had been glazed, and on the other outer wall a new window had been made, an elegant, arched window with latticed panes. She could see Llanglyn far below in the valley, its lights blurred by the rain. Gwynneth went to draw the curtains, bobbing another nervous curtsey.

Mally smiled, gathering her own scattered senses at last. "Have you been a lady's maid before, Gwynneth?"

"No, ma'am."

"Have you been here long?"

"Two months, ma'am. I came when my mam heard they wanted someone up here."

Mally sat down before the old-fashioned dressing table. "Unpin my hair, if you please, Gwynneth."

"Yes, ma'am."

The maid fumbled awkwardly, and Mally smiled at her in the mirror. "Don't be afraid, Gwynneth, I shall not bite you."

"No, but I think Lady Annabel might."

Mally laughed. "No, she won't."

"I nearly dropped when *Mishur* Louis said as I was to attend you both; I thought you were bringing your own maids with you." The girl's Welsh accent was melodic.

"Lucy wouldn't come because she and my mother do not see eye to eye with Mr. Vallender. So, you see, Lady Annabel and I are more than glad to have you look after us."

"They're all wrong about Mr. Vallender, ma'am. He's kind, more kind than anyone I know. And handsome enough to whip the devil's tail." The maid blushed.

Mally said nothing. The girl was right, Richard Vallender could whip the devil's tail ten times over—

Gwynneth finished unpinning her hair and then unhooked the gown with great care. "Oh, such a lovely gown, ma'am, I think it must be wonderful to wear something like this. *Mawreddog.*"

"If you think *that's* grand, wait until you see Lady Annabel's toggery."

Gwynneth smiled. "She's an earl's daughter, isn't she?"

"Yes. A title as long as my arm. Gwynneth, what do you know of this business with Abel?" Mally slipped into her wrap, tying it slowly around her waist.

"Abel? Oh, it's all so wrong, you know. Abel wouldn't do anything to an old lady like that, he's as gentle as my sister's pet lamb."

Mally watched the way the girl avoided her eyes. "Is there anyone else staying here, Gwynneth? A lady?"

"No, ma'am. There's just yourself, Lady Annabel, and Sir Christopher staying here."

Mally brushed her hair thoughtfully. She'd get nothing more out of the maid. But Abel had definitely thought for a moment that it had been Maria in the courtyard—"Where is Lady Annabel now, Gwynneth?" She changed the subject.

"Still in the solar with Sir Christopher, I believe." The maid smiled shyly, biting her lip. "I got it wrong, you know. I thought *you* were to marry Sir Christopher, not Lady Annabel."

Mally turned. "I am, Gwynneth."

The maid's eyes widened. "Oh—I—"

"Getting on well, were they?"

"Oh, ma'am!" Gwynneth looked as if she wished the floor would open and swallow her, and her hands were shaking.

Mally put her hand on her arm. "It's all right, Gwynneth, you haven't stepped out of line."

"Oh, ma'am, I could cut my tongue!"

"Don't do anything so drastic, please." Mally continued brushing her hair, pondering what Gwynneth might have seen in the solar. Had Annabel been fairly stampeding over that lost ground then?

Someone knocked at the door and Gwynneth opened it. Chris stood there, his face set. Gwynneth took one look at him and scuttled out, closing the door behind her.

Mally turned. "Chris."

He looked around, his glance falling immediately on Richard's coat. "I trust you enjoyed your *tête-à-tête* with Richard."

"As much as you enjoyed yours with Annabel, I would imagine." She held his gaze.

"And what was it he had to show you? His memories?"

Her chin came up stubbornly. "No, as a matter of fact they was *my* memories! Mine and Daniel's. And if you don't like to hear that name then I am sorry." She put the brush down angrily.

"No doubt you found it most enjoyable."

She thought for a moment. Richard was right, she wasn't facing her decisions. Slowly she took the ring from her finger. "Enjoyable? Yes, Chris, I did, more enjoyable than I find most of my time spent with you now. Take the ring, give it to Annabel, for she is the one who should wear it, not me."

He stared at the ring. "Is that your final word?"

"Yes, I would rather spend my life alone dwelling on the past, than with you continually arguing and misunderstanding."

"But you won't be alone, will you? You'll be with my good friend Richard!"

She shook her head. "This has nothing to do with him really, Chris. It's been on the cards ever since we were foolish enough to become engaged in the first place." She took his hand and pressed the ring into his palm, closing his fingers gently over it. "I love you very much, Chris, but we should remain what we always have been, the very best of friends. We are killing that friendship and love at this moment, aren't we? Look at me, Chris, look at me and admit that I am right."

He met her eyes, and then bent his head, brushing his lips over hers. "I know, Mally, I know. But *I* do love *you* as much as was needed, you know that, don't you?"

She lowered her eyes. "You did, Chris, for a long time.

But not anymore. And don't be at odds with Richard over this, for it isn't his fault."

"Isn't it?"

"No."

He glanced at the coat again, and then back into her eyes. "I wish you well, Mally, my love." He put his hand to the nape of her neck and drew her lips toward his again.

She touched the hand holding the ring. "Give the ring to Annabel, Chris."

"Is that where my happiness lies then?"

"You tell me, Chris." She smiled.

As the door closed behind him she turned to look at her reflection in the tall cheval glass. She felt so weary—

Gwynneth tapped timidly on the door. "Shall I do anything else, ma'am?"

"No, thank you. Do you know where Lady Annabel is?"

"Gone to her room, ma'am. I'm to attend her now."

Mally smiled. "She's no doubt tired out with her ghostly searchings for Lady Jacquetta. Amongst other things."

"Lady Jacquetta? Haven't you seen her then?"

Mally stared at the maid's surprised face. "No. Have you?"

"Oh, *Duw*, yes, the first moment I came here. I always see them if they're there, and *she's* there right enough."

"What's she like?"

"Well—she's sort of *watery*. Gray and floaty. Like gossamer." Gwynneth blushed. "You don't think I'm—?"

"Fey? Probably. Go on."

"Well, that's it really, she moves around the castle a lot. Up in the south tower, the gallery in the great hall, and down in the dungeon sometimes, but then that's where Sir Francis put her first off, isn't it?"

"I don't know, Gwynneth."

"Oh, there is something else. She never shows her hands. Never once, they're always hidden away. Almost—well, almost as if they aren't there anymore."

Mally shuddered. What was it Annabel had said. Tearing with her bloodied hands?

"Shall I go then, ma'am?"

"Yes, Gwynneth. *Nos da.*"

"*Nos da,* ma'am."

"Oh, and Gwynneth. Don't tell Lady Annabel you've seen her precious ghost, she'll never forgive you."

"No, ma'am." Puzzled, the maid closed the door.

Mally sat on the bed, looking down at her ringless finger. Annabel had won. She took a long, soothing breath. Or had common sense, perhaps, been the victor?

Chapter 22

The wind continued to rise during the night, and Mally lay in a fitful sleep on the bed, still in her wrap. The fire flared and glowed with each gust of the gale, and the room was warm. With a great gasp, the storm raged again, flinging itself against the ancient fortress as if angry at the resistance. The window burst open with a crash, banging loudly and setting the curtains fluttering.

Mally sat up with a start, the wind catching at her hair and dragging it across her face. With a great effort she closed the window. Through the deep embrasure of the wall she could see the ravaged hillside where the trees bent and swayed. A horse-chestnut had fallen, torn up by its roots to lie across the drive, and the smaller, lighter rowan trees seemed almost to bend to the ground as they gave before the onslaught. Down in the valley several lights burned in Llanglyn, nervous lights for those afraid of the autumn storm. She watched the night for a while and then made to draw the curtains. But something caught her eye.

Lights were moving down by the lodge and a horseman was riding back up toward the castle. It was Richard Vallender. What secrets did he have? She watched him, certain that Maria was here at Castell Melyn. For a tiny moment her mind went back to the dungeon, and to the warm softness of his lips over hers— As he passed from sight into the courtyard, she left the bedroom and stepped into the chilly passage outside. From a window overlooking the courtyard she could see the light still burning up in the south tower. At the foot of the tower was a door, a small flight of stone steps leading up to it. She heard the clatter of Richard's horse beneath the barbican, although she could not see him. Then, suddenly, a woman was standing at the top of the stone steps by the tower.

Abel came from the barbican, and Mally pushed the stiff catch of the window to open it. The sound of the storm was stronger up here than it had been down in the courtyard, but still she could hear Abel's voice.

"Mas' Vallender, Miss Maria want you."

Maria. Mally stared at the woman on the steps. Yes, it was Maria, her wild hair blowing freely, without a pin or a mobcap to restrain it, and a yellow gown which flapped and fluttered, revealing petticoats which were heavy with lace.

Richard came from the door of the chapel and hurried across to the steps, running up them two at a time. He caught Maria's hands and she looked up at him. She seemed to be crying, Mally thought, and Richard pulled her close, holding her tightly, stroking the thick black hair gently. Then he pushed the door of the tower open and he and Maria went inside, closing the door behind them.

Mally closed the window and then leaned her forehead against the cold glass. There could be no doubt now. Maria was here, and Richard Vallender had known all along. And Maria was not ill. Mally thought of returning to her bed, but there would be no point, for she knew she would not sleep now. No, she knew where Maria was, and she intended facing her sister now, even if it was—she glanced at the clock on the wall above the gatehouse—even if it was three o'clock in the morning.

She hurried along the passageway toward the stairs, which were icy cold beneath her feet. The solar was in darkness as she glanced across the courtyard at it from a window opposite. The door at the foot of the steps was heavy and the rain's noise was immediate as she pulled it open. All around she could hear the storm, but still down in the courtyard it was fairly calm, like the eye of a hurricane.

Her bare feet slipped occasionally on the cobbles, and she was concentrating on keeping her balance and did not see Abel until he caught her arm.

"No, miss—"

She put her hand on the rail at the foot of the south tower. "My sister is in there, Abel, let me go."

"No, miss. Mas' Vallender—"

"Can go to the devil! Release me, Abel!" Mally tried to pull her arm away.

"Let her go, Abel." Richard stood at the top of the steps.

Abel obeyed immediately, and Mally began to climb the steps, but Richard came down to meet her and seized her more roughly than Abel had. He steered her back down the steps and across the courtyard.

"She's in there! Take your hands off me!" she cried, struggling.

He said nothing, but kept dragging her across the cobbles. She slipped and lost her balance, but the strength of his grip was such that he kept her from falling, his fingers digging into her arm and bruising her.

In the buttery he released her. She stood there, rubbing her arm. "I saw her, damn you!" she cried. "And you cannot bluff me otherwise this time!"

"There'll be a fire in the solar—"

"No doubt, but I shall not be diverted!"

"You pick your moments for your grand gestures, madam! Now, *if* you please—go up to the solar!"

She considered defying him, but there was something in his eyes. She turned, hurrying up past Gillian Vallender's portrait and the grandfather clock, and then up the winding stone steps to the solar.

It was dark inside, and the glow of the dying fire was the only light. Richard closed the door and leaned back against it for a moment, looking at her as she stood by the wide black fireplace.

"You lied to me tonight," she said at last.

"No, I did not. If you recall, I said that there was nothing I *could* tell you. And that was so. Then. But now that you have seen her—"

"I have seen her and I know that you lied to me before, when you said that you didn't know where she was. How *could* you be so callous? How could *either* of you be so callous? Just a small note would have sufficed, anything but that dreadful silence and not knowing anything."

"There is a reason."

"No doubt."

He turned sharply. "Sarcasm ill becomes you at times, Mally! If I tell you there is a reason, then that is so! Do I make myself clear?"

She drew her wrap nervously around her. "Yes."

"Thank you, madam. Now then, how much one of them are you?" He gestured in the direction of Llanglyn.

"I don't understand."

"Don't you? You were mightily determined to come here, weren't you?"

"And you equally as determined to keep me away!" she countered. "But then *you* have a *reason*, don't you?"

He sighed. "Mally," he said, a little more gently, "I must know. Are you sent here?"

She stared. "I am not sent at all. I come of my own volition, because I sense that you know something of my sister. That is my sole reason, that and nothing else."

He smiled then. "I am more glad than you can realize. Now, I will tell you. Maria is here, you saw her, and she has been here since she left a false trail leading to London."

"And back to Cirencester, Gloucester, and Hereford."

His eyes flickered. "You know that much, do you?"

"I'm her sister, damn you. Did you imagine I would sit back and play the flute while she gaily vanished into oblivion?"

"No, but I had not imagined you to be so tenacious, either. You discovered that much of our trail, which I am surprised at."

"Our trail? So it was you in the phaeton?"

"Yes."

"You must have swept her from her feet, that is all I can say." Mally looked away at the fire.

"Me?" He was laughing. "I've never swept Maria from anywhere, let alone her feet. And neither has *she* stopped *my* breath. There is nothing of that sort between your sister and me, Mally, although I suppose you may be forgiven for believing there was."

"Then why is she here with you?" she asked.

"Because Andrew York is here."

"That is a tasteless attempt at humor, for Andrew York is dead. And buried."

"A coffin of stones is buried. But Andrew is alive, or half alive." He poured two glasses from the decanter on the silver tray. "And it is on his account that I went to London to see Stiller. And on his account that I tried—politely—to keep you from coming here. You are of Llanglyn."

"And that is a crime?"

He pushed a glass into her hand. "I have good reason to mistrust *anyone* from down in that valley. Anyone. We believe that Andrew witnessed the murder that night, and that is why we pretended to bury him—with Nathaniel's constant help of course—to give him the chance of recovering so that he could point a finger at the guilty man. Or men."

"Perhaps he will point it at Abel. Abel *was* in Llanglyn that night, wasn't he?"

"Yes. But he did not kill anyone."

"How can you be so sure?"

"Because, Mally, he says he did not, and that is sufficient for me. Abel does not lie."

"Not even to save his own neck?"

"He would not do anything which would require such a lie, Mally. Believe me."

"Then what happened that night, as far as you know?"

He indicated a chair. "I cannot sit until you do, Mally, and I'm too weary to stand for little reason." She sat down and he slumped heavily on the sofa opposite, leaning his head back and running his hand through his dark hair. "Andrew and Abel went to Llanglyn because Andrew had arranged a meeting with Maria at Nathaniel's house. Nathaniel, however, was not back from a patient when they arrived, so Abel left Andrew waiting at the top of the steps by the house. He rode back across the ford to your mother's house, to the bottom of the lane by that break in the wall. Maria was waiting there with her horse and they began to ride back toward the town. It was a stormy night much like tonight. As they reached the front of the courthouse they saw Andrew riding at breakneck speed toward the ford, pursued by some men on horseback. Abel caught the bridle of your sister's horse and they hid beneath the gateway of the house, completely hidden by shadow. They saw one of the pursuing men apparently use a sling—"

"Jacob Turney."

"No one saw who it was, but the younger Turney *is*

renowned for his skill, isn't he? Anyway, his aim was excellent, for the stone caught Andrew's temple and he fell forward in the saddle, but did not fall from the horse, which took fright and galloped across the ford and up here to the castle. Abel kept Maria in the shadows of the entrance and they saw the men halt, apparently satisfied that they had killed Andrew. From the courthouse they could not make out a single face among those on the other side of the river, Mally."

"Did Abel and Maria believe Andrew had been killed too?"

"Yes. And no doubt they would have been pursued themselves had not Abel had the wit to hide. When all was clear, he made Maria return to her mother, and then went up the lane. Which was when Brew Darril saw him. So, the murderer or murderers knew that Abel had been seen in Llanglyn *before* the murder, when he rode to collect Maria, and that he was still abroad *after* the murder. With Andrew disposed of, Abel was the perfect scapegoat. The only Negro in Llanglyn, in Breconshire probably, and from the disliked Castell Melyn. He must have seemed heaven-sent."

Richard loosened his cravat and tossed it to the floor, unbuttoning his shirt a little. "Andrew had already been brought back by his horse, and then when Abel came later with his tale, he wondered what had happened in Llanglyn. Nathaniel came up the following morning to apologize to Andrew for not having been at home, and of course he had the whole tale of Mrs. Harmon's murder. We put two and two together, that from his vantage point on those steps Andrew would have seen whoever came out of the old lady's house."

"And from the matter of the sling, and their trouble-stirring since, you think it is Jasper and his cronies?"

"Yes. Nathaniel and I decided that there was a chance

Andrew would recover, and so we set about deceiving Jasper. And everyone else."

"Hence the false funeral and the strenuous denials that Abel was in Llanglyn. But that last was surely a mistake, for he was seen by honest folk as well."

"I know. But to admit that he *was* in Llanglyn would have meant his arrest, and I was not prepared to allow that. I used my position as a gentleman and landowner, etcetera etcetera, to convince those in authority that *I* was the one who was speaking truthfully. And Nathaniel backed me up. He said that as he was the only doctor for many a mile, he would be safe enough, and he was right."

"So now I know what Dr. Towers said to Maria that day—until he came she had believed Andrew York was dead."

He nodded. "But the rest of your sister's activities were entirely her own fool notion! She put a letter to me beneath Nathaniel's door, telling me to come to Cirencester to bring her secretly back here. She wanted to be with Andrew at all costs, and by the time I received the letter she was well on her way. To say that I was furious would surely be to put it excessively mildly. If she had remained at the courthouse and then attended the false funeral looking suitably heart-broken, I'm sure we could have convinced Jasper that he was safe. Instead of which he's uneasy. Andrew and Abel were in Llanglyn that night, outside Nathaniel's house. That always meant that Andrew was meeting Maria—everyone in Llanglyn knew that. Maria's disappearance like that made Jasper Turney think that she too may have seen something."

"That's why he followed her! *Jasper* is the unknown country man at the Swan with Two Necks." Mally explained about Mr. Paulington and about the intruder in her bedroom.

"Well, what you've told me now only convinces me that I'm right. Jasper thinks Maria is a witness against him." He smiled. "And perhaps you can guess now why I was so eager to prevent you coming here. I thought Jasper might put two and two together and think you had come to be with Maria."

She watched the glow of the firelight passing through a cut crystal glass. "And you didn't trust me anyway, that's more to the point, isn't it?"

He reached across and took her hand. "Please don't think that. No, I thought you believed in Abel's guilt, for if people like your mother believe it, I had no reason to think you would be any different. For which lack of trust, forgive me."

"I forgive you everything—now. And I must have your forgiveness too, for I have been guilty of black thoughts concerning you."

"That I have been harboring your sister here for my own ends?"

"Yes." She met his eyes. "Yes, I thought that."

"What a fickle, nimble soul you must think me, giving shelter to your sister and then making advances to you."

She flushed.

His thumb soothed her palm. "I deserve your black thoughts, perhaps."

"If you had told me the truth that day in Hyde Park, I would have believed you then. Instead you told me lies, and I *knew* you were lying."

"I was—except in the advice I offered concerning foolish, ill-thought-out marriages."

She took her hand away. "That has been resolved." Before he could say anything more, she went on. "What was it that brought Abel into Llanglyn yesterday at such risk to his own life?"

"Andrew moved his hand. Oh, it sounds nothing, but until then he had not moved a muscle. Maria sits up there in that tower with him night and day, talking and coaxing him, pushing spoonfuls of broth down his throat and holding his hand. But there is no response. He lies there, motionless, for all the world as if he is asleep. Until yesterday. Gwynneth had brought a tray of food and she was leaving, when she lost her balance on the steep, winding steps. She fell down three or four steps before she managed to catch the rail and hold on. She screamed, because for a moment she thought she was going to fall right to the foot of the tower. At the sound of the scream, Andrew's hand clenched. And that was it, nothing more."

"So, he's not beyond all hope, is he? He reacted to something."

"But to what? Gwynneth's scream? We thought of that, and yesterday afternoon when Chris was still down at the courthouse with you, we tried it out. Gwynneth screamed again, but to no avail. Whatever it was about her original scream could not be reproduced to the same effect. If it *was* the scream."

"And nothing else has happened since?"

"Yes. Tonight. When Maria called me he had just reacted to something again. She was almost asleep by his bedside when something woke her with a start, a spider crawled over her hand. A very large, hairy spider, according to Maria."

She smiled. "Every spider merits that description, if you listen to Maria. She's terrified of them. Perhaps that's it, Richard. Fear. There are screams and screams, but a scream of fear is quite different."

"And it is also the one thing which cannot be made up, isn't it?"

"I know." She sighed. "Perhaps if we tell Chris and Annabel *they* can help."

"Aye, well, perhaps the time *has* come for honesty all around."

"Does Maria know I'm here?"

"Yes. She knows and she has wanted to see you from the outset, but I'm afraid I persuaded her against it." He smiled faintly. "My mistrustful nature coming to the fore again, I fear."

"I'm flattered to have brought about such a strong reaction."

"You, Mally, have brought about a very definite reaction in me, I do assure you."

She looked at him in the firelight. No woman could remain indifferent to him, not even Annabel, who found the need to flirt a little with him even in front of Chris. There was something about Richard Vallender—

She smiled at him. "Can I see Maria now?"

"Backing down from an interesting conversation, Mally?"

"Yes."

He nodded. "Maria it is then. Come on."

Chapter 23

The room in the tower was sparsely furnished. Two plain beds stood against the walls, and between them a small chest of drawers on which was a candlestick which dripped molten wax. Droplets fell into the dished base, congealing into a thick, rippled pool, and the flame swayed as Richard opened the door.

Maria was sitting on a low chair beside one of the beds, holding the hand of the man who lay there. He was young and good-looking, and Mally could see immediately the likeness between him and the portrait of his cousin, Gillian Vallender. His fair hair was longer than was fashionable, but its length suited him, emphasizing his almost boyish looks. His eyes were closed, but Mally knew that if they were open they would be a very bright blue, as Richard had said. A bandage was around his head, fresh and white, and he wore a dressing gown of donkey-brown wool.

Maria got to her feet, her eyes glittering with tears as she saw Mally. "You told her, Richard. Oh, I'm so glad—" She ran to Mally, flinging her arms around her and holding her tightly. "I so wanted you, Mally, I needed you desperately."

"It's all right now, Maria, don't cry." Mally smoothed the wild black hair lovingly. "Sweeting, we've worried so about you."

"I *had* to be with him, I just *had* to. I love him more than anything else in the world and I wasn't going to stay down with Mother. I didn't want to lie to her—"

"So you didn't say anything at all. A lie would have been better almost. Anyway, it doesn't matter now." Mally sat on the end of the empty bed. "Are you all right?"

"Yes. Perfectly."

"You know what I mean, Maria."

"Dr. Towers told you!"

"No, he didn't. I'm your sister, I just *knew*. *Are* you all right?"

Maria glanced at Richard and Mally could see that it was obviously the first inkling he had had of Maria's condition. "Yes, Mally, I'm ridiculously all right. When Andrew recovers I shall marry him, Mally, no matter how engaged I am to Thomas Clevely *or* how opposed Mother is to the match!"

"I should hope so. I am to be an aunt and I want everything to be perfectly legal and aboveboard! Mother'll approve anyway, under the circumstances." *Please God, let him recover*— Mally looked at the silent, motionless figure in the other bed.

Maria went to him, taking his hand and sitting beside him. "If only he'd be himself again. Yesterday when Gwynneth screamed, I really thought— But then it was gone, as quickly as it had come."

Richard put his hand gently on her shoulder. "And tonight, Maria? What happened tonight?"

"Just as I told you. The spider on my hand roused me—"

"Did you gasp? Scream? Anything like that?"

"I don't know, I was so drowsy. Why?"

"Mally thinks it could be fear which makes him react." Richard's fingers stroked her soothingly, and Mally could see how it calmed her, for she trembled very slightly all the time. How tired she looked, with huge dark rings under her eyes. And her face was so pale. Gone was the bright, vivacious Maria she had last seen months before. "When did you last sleep, Maria?" Richard asked gently.

"Earlier. I don't know. I'm afraid to in case he needs me—"

"Let me have one of the maids sit here with him while you sleep in the bed which was put there for you." He turned her face toward him, his hand firmly beneath her chin. "Listen to me now—you do yourself no good at all by making yourself stay awake, and you'll do Andrew no good in the long run either. Or the baby. Do you hear me?"

Maria nodded, touching his hand briefly and smiling. "I do not know what I should have done without you, Richard."

"I know what *I* should have done without *you*, madam. A good deal better than I have done!"

She pulled a wry face which was a ghost of her former self. "I know. I'm sorry."

"So, you will take something to eat and then behave yourself by going to sleep?"

"Yes, Richard. I promise. But you will have someone sit with him, someone trustworthy who won't doze off the moment I do?"

"I promise."

Maria stood, crossing to the window. "What was happening down at the lodge earlier? I heard the dog and saw the lights."

"Tom's terrier set up a clamor about something. A fox in the chickens, probably. Anyway, by the time I got down there there was nothing. Don't look so wide-eyed, Maria, no one can get in here without being seen."

"I know. But at night it's always worse. And I *feel* that Jasper is agitated now. *Really* agitated."

"That's because you are," said Richard reassuringly, avoiding Mally's eyes. "Now then, I shall have a maid bring some food while you prepare yourself for bed."

"Shall you tell Chris? I know he's here. With Lady Annabel Murchison."

Richard nodded. "Yes, Mally and I will tell them. Over breakfast."

He left, and Maria allowed Mally to unhook the yellow gown. "I'm so weary, Mally—"

"You're silly, not sleeping or eating."

"I just couldn't, it felt like neglecting him." Maria looked at him again and Mally saw the great love in her eyes. "Oh, if you only knew him as I do, Mally. He's everything I could ever want."

"Except rich."

"Well, we can't all snare Chris Carlyon, can we?" Maria caught her hand, intending to wave the engagement ring before her. But there was only a white mark on Mally's finger. "What's happened, Mally?"

"There isn't going to be a Carlyon marriage for me, Maria."

"Why?"

"Let's just say we both realized we were making a mistake."

Maria looked at her. "Let's perhaps just say *you* realized you were making a mistake. Chris would go on making that particular mistake *ad infinitum,* wouldn't he?"

"I doubt it—he was fast coming to the end of his patience with me."

"So, Annabel wins after all?"

Mally shrugged. "I don't know. I hope so, for she's

been more than faithful. And he *is* happy in her company."

"I always liked her. It was a shame that Chris dropped her so unkindly in order to take you up after Daniel died."

"He thought she should be left in no doubt."

"Well, let's hope he more than makes up for his past mistakes now. You don't mind that it's over?"

"No. Mother will, though."

Maria groaned. "Oh, *what* a pair we are—there's me disgracing myself with Andrew, and you throwing over the Carlyon match. Mother will throw a fit of the vapors to end *all* fits of the vapors. Poor Mother—"

Mally helped her into the cold, hard bed. "Now then, Maria Berrisford, you are to eat and then sleep, do you hear me?"

"I hear you. Mally, I *do* love Andrew, you know."

"I know, sweeting."

Mally kissed her and left the room as a maid came up carrying a tray. At the door she glanced back at Maria's tired, pale face, and then at the motionless figure in the other bed. Not by one flicker did Andrew York seem to be even vaguely alive—

Outside, the courtyard was deserted. The storm howled out beyond the walls, but the courtyard was like the eye of a hurricane. High above she became aware of the flag cracking and flapping on the flagpole above the keep. She shivered, her wrap damp from the rain. Lucy would moan of pneumonia, or worse— She smiled, remembering Lucy's anxious, last-minute plea that she and Annabel should not come to the castle.

To Richard Vallender's castle. She stopped, looking around the stark wet stone walls. Castell Melyn meant Richard Vallender now. As she stood there in the cold darkness she knew that that thought had been at the back of her mind all along, and it had nothing to do with

Maria's disappearance. She had pursued everything because of Maria, but with a willingness born of her own interest in Richard.

She went through the buttery and stood for a long time looking at Gillian Vallender's portrait. The soft colors and brushwork glowed in the lamplight. For the first time Mally really understood Chris's jealousy over the renaming of Vimiero House.

Gillian's portrait was still here, still in a place where everyone would see her—

Chapter 24

Annabel closed the door of the dining room, and Chris turned from contemplating the fire roaring in the hearth.

"We appear to be the first hungry souls stirring this morning," he said.

She removed her heavy woolen shawl and went closer to the warmth, holding her hands out. "I slept like the proverbial log, you know. By the look of my bed this morning I did not move once! There's hardly a crease."

"Would that I could say the same thing."

She looked at him. "That sounds heartfelt. What's wrong?"

"Mally and I are no longer engaged."

Annabel left the fire, walking slowly to the dining-room table and surveying the shining silver cutlery and gold and white plates. There was a smell of coffee in the air, and toast, and bacon. And chrysanthemums, from the elegant porcelain dish in the center of the table. She looked at the flowers, so crisp and clear, a mass of cream and bronze. She hardly dared breathe. It was over between Chris and Mally?

Chris watched her, taking in the prettily piled golden curls with their silly, elaborate comb and plume, and the shining, smooth apple-green gown. Was Mally right? Did his happiness, and Annabel's, lie in their marriage?

"Annabel?"

"Yes?"

"Well, say something, even if it's only a comment on the weather."

"I was trying to think of what to say. Did Mally end it?"

"Yes."

"Not because of my behavior last night?" Annabel turned suddenly, "Oh, please say it wasn't that, for I know I behaved badly."

"No more badly than I did. Anyway, it wasn't because of you."

"Then what?"

He pursed his lips thoughtfully. "I rather fancy Richard had said something to make up her mind. Not that it made any difference. In the long run she would have ended it anyway. I know that."

"I'm so sorry, Chris, truly I am, for I know how you love her."

He smiled then. "I felt sorry for myself at first, I will admit, but now— She's right, it was hopeless. We make better friends than lovers."

"So, you're not sorry now?"

"No."

"Good." Annabel's eyes shone as she smiled.

The door opened and Richard came in. "Alone, *mes enfants*? What manner of host am I to so neglect you?"

Annabel raised her eyebrows. "A poor one."

"Well, I am here to entertain you with my blistering repartee and dazzling charm."

"Oh, spare us," groaned Chris. "Where's Mally? I'm dying of hunger."

"She will not be too long, I fancy," said Richard, drawing a chair out for Annabel, "but she did not sleep too well last night."

"And how would you know?" asked Annabel.

"Because—dreadful as it might sound—I was with her for part of the time."

Annabel looked quickly at Chris. "Yes, it does sound dreadful. Why were you together, or is that an embarrassing question?"

Richard smiled as he unfolded a napkin. "No, it isn't embarrassing. Would that it were."

Chris nodded. "I rather think you mean that."

"I do. To be caught *in flagrante delicto* with the delightful Mally would do my overweening male pride a great deal of good. Unfortunately, I cannot lay claim to such notoriety."

"*Yet*," finished Annabel, taking her own napkin. "Oh, come on, Mally!"

As if in answer, the door opened and Mally came in, her flounced turquoise satin skirts rustling. "I'm sorry if I have kept you all waiting."

"Not at all," said Annabel. "I have had a vastly pleasing morning so far."

"I'll warrant you have," said Mally, smiling as Richard drew her chair out. "Undoubtedly the best you've had in a long, long time, eh, Annabel?"

"I cannot deny it."

Chris lifted a silver-domed dish and inspected the mixed grill steaming there. "Mouth-watering indeed. What is your desire ladies? As long as you leave me some of those kidneys, I will serve you whatever you wish."

"Then we'll have the kidneys," said Annabel, smiling.

"*Chienne*. You don't even like kidneys." Chris smiled as he forked some bacon and beefsteak onto her plate.

Annabel was determined not to let Richard's earlier

words pass without further comment. "Now then, why were you two up together last night? What have Chris and I been missing?"

"You tell them," said Mally to Richard.

"More and more mysterious," said Chris, offering some bacon to Mally, who shook her head. "What's it about?"

"Mally's lost sister. The man she wants to marry. And the murder down in Llanglyn." Richard put his fingertips together thoughtfully.

Annabel's knife dropped with a clatter. "Is that all? I thought it would be *interesting!*"

"It is interesting. Shall I begin?"

Annabel nodded. "It's like a bedtime story at nanny's knee again. Will *you* slap my wrist if I suck my thumb?"

"I shall indeed, it's a disgusting habit."

Richard poured himself some black coffee, and began to tell them all about Andrew, Maria, and the death of Mrs. Harmon.

Annabel's bacon and beefsteak lay cold and untouched when he at last finished, and Chris had not even got around to putting anything on his own plate. Mally stared at the bowl of chrysanthemums.

Annabel took a long breath. "That odious Turney fellow, I *knew* he was up to no good the moment I set eyes on him, but I didn't imagine he had done anything quite so despicable as to murder that old lady in her bed."

"Wait now," said Chris, "we have no proof that it *was* Turney. Someone who's expert with a sling *could* be his brother Jacob, or it could be someone else. And it could also be that Turney *genuinely* believes Abel is guilty. It seems to me that all your accusations are guesswork. If Turney thinks Maria saw him and that she is up here, why hasn't he tried to find out?"

"How?" asked Richard. "It's not possible to get into Castell Melyn from the outside, I've seen to that. The lodge drawbridge is raised every night and Tom's hounds roam the grounds."

"Tom?"

"The lodgekeeper. A very thorough fellow." Richard smiled. "So, Jasper Turney would find it difficult to discover if Maria Berrisford is here—none of the people I employ go down into Llanglyn. All provisions are purchased in Abergavenny or Hereford, and I employ no one from Llanglyn itself."

Chris looked doubtful. "I still think it unlikely Turney is guilty."

Annabel frowned. "Well, *I* think Richard and Mally are right."

"Why? Have *you* a good reason, or merely a feeling?"

"A good reason. Turney is the one who's been whipping up feeling, and that points to needing a scapegoat—Abel. The poor man is the ideal subject upon which to center all the mistrust and superstition. And there's something else, something I heard during my first week here when we couldn't leave the house because of the weather. Pattie said that the first person to discover Mrs. Harmon's body was Mrs. Turney. Mrs. Turney, who'd never been a particular friend of the old lady, and yet who took it into her head to take a basket of fruit to her at nearly midnight! That basket takes a little bit of swallowing. I'll warrant Jasper was just making sure the murder was discovered while Abel was still around, and if the unpleasant Brew Darril had seen Abel, then it was worth the try. *And* I think that Turney now thinks Maria saw them at the old lady's house too, and that's why he came to London and to Mally's house."

Chris pursed his lips. "All right, I'll grant you there is a good deal of circumstantial evidence—"

Mally looked at him. "Circumstantial? Then why did he come to London?"

"How do you know it *was* him?"

"I just do."

"There you are," said Chris, "it's still guesswork. Richard, why didn't you take the wretched Andrew to Stiller instead of leaving him here? Surely you could have got him out without the whole of Llanglyn knowing?"

"We could have, if it had not been for both Nathaniel and Stiller advising against moving him. I begin to weary of it all now—"

Mally looked quickly at him. "Don't say that."

"Well, I must be honest. I don't think we shall get anywhere with Andrew. There is nothing I would like more than to be able to prove Turney's guilt and to have Andrew well once more. But I do not think either will happen."

"But Andrew's hand moved—"

"Mally," said Chris, "an animal will twitch even after death. Andrew's hand probably moved because of some nerve, that's all."

"But if it *was* a real reaction?"

Richard lowered his eyes. "If it was, then there is still some hope."

Annabel stood, crossing to the window to look out. "And there is still only circumstantial evidence of a very vague kind for any court of law. If there was something *solid*."

"Such as?" asked Chris, leaning back in his chair to look at her. "A letter of confession?"

"Don't be sarcastic. I don't know what, do I? Anyway, we should go to see Maria and Andrew, don't you think? Perhaps *seeing* him—"

There was a knock at the door and Louis entered, bowing as he stood aside for Dr. Towers to come in.

"Good morning, ladies, gentlemen. Oh, driving in this weather is hardly a relaxing exercise."

Richard ushered him to a seat. "Then take some breakfast with us and recover, my friend. What brings you up here so early?"

"Well—" The doctor glanced around the room doubtfully.

"It's all right, Nathaniel, they know all about it. Has something happened?" Richard's smile faded as he sensed Nathaniel's unease.

"Well, yes, something has, Richard. Last night Jasper, Jacob, and Brew Darril opened the grave."

"You are sure?"

"I *saw* them, Richard. I sat up for two hours or more, freezing to the bone, watching from the attic window. They opened it, inspected the coffin, and then closed it all up again."

Chris smiled. "There's your proof, Richard. They could only have one reason for looking in that grave."

"They could be robbing graves. I understand there is a demand for bodies for medical purposes," pointed out Annabel.

"Bodies over a month old are hardly suitable unless a skeleton is required. Even the most dedicated hospital would be put off by a moldering body."

"Don't," she said, looking slightly sick.

Richard glanced at Nathaniel. "You didn't think of getting someone else to witness it with you, did you?"

"Oh, yes, I know that my word is to be doubted at the moment. I roused my housekeeper from her bed and she saw it too. You have two witnesses, Richard."

"We must hope that this is enough then."

"It should be," said Chris. "Anyway, *I* shall go to the fort at Abergavenny. It's quite surprising how much weight a mere title has. I shall sally forth in the landau looking my most splendid."

"I shall come with you. Two titles are better than one."

Annabel turned from the window to smile at him.

"Think of the impropriety," he pointed out.

"I am," she rejoined. "With luck I might even be compromised."

Mally laughed. "Oh, Annabel, you deserve him, truly you do—"

Chris flushed, but he was smiling. "Very well, Lady Annabel, come with me."

"At my peril?"

"No. At mine."

Later that morning the landau moved slowly down the lane, passing over snapped twigs and torn leaves. The trees shuddered as the gale gusted relentlessly, and their branches scratched over the top of the carriage. Above, the heavy clouds still scudded low over the Black Mountains, hiding the summits in a veil of mist and rain. At the foot of the hill the coachman halted the team of roans as the doctor's pony and trap came splashing across the ford toward it. Chris leaned out.

Unseen, behind the thick hedge with its drapes of old man's beard, Brew Darril was setting a rabbit snare. He crept closer, listening to what was being said.

"What is it, Dr. Towers?" asked Chris.

"The stagecoach has just come in, Sir Christopher. The Abergavenny road's blocked by two or three fallen trees—they caught the storm badly up there."

"Damn. Is there another ford? Hereford perhaps?"

"Yes, that's the nearest, but it's further—"

"It will have to do. Thank you for coming."

"I thought I'd miss you. Well, good luck, Sir Christopher. Lady Annabel."

The landau lurched on again, and Brew ran his long fingers slowly over the snare. Then he set it carefully by the burrow, concealing it with leaves and grass.

Jasper poured three mugs of strong ale and pushed them across the table. "You sure, Brew?"

"I 'eard what I 'eard. There en't no mistake. I knowed as that damned leech was watchin' last night, it was a fool notion to look in the grave."

"I 'ad to know. Once and fer all."

"Well, now you knows and look where it's got us, an' all."

Jasper turned on him. "You pickin' faults, my fine lad? Eh?"

"No." Brew backed down immediately. "It's just—well, we didn't need any more proof, did we? That fancy Miss Mally 'ave gone scuttlin' up there, we guessed as 'er sister's up there an' all." Jasper glanced around the tap room. "I thought as she was in Lunnon, mind, I could 'ave swore it were 'er in that window. Can't tell them Berrisford wenches apart sometimes. Any road, we're damned sure they'm both up at the castle now. On top of that we *know* as the leech and Vallender 'ave lied 'bout the black feller. I thought as the wench was all we needed 'ave worried over, but if York *en't* dead—"

"He may be alive, Jasper," said Brew thoughtfully, "but there must be sommat diddicky wi' 'en—why else 'ave that leech been cuttin' a furrow 'twixt here and there, eh?"

Jasper turned savagely on his younger brother. "Call yourself a slingman, our Jacob? Damn fool I was to trust the likes of you."

"It weren't my fault!"

"Never is. Any road, Brew, did you find what you'd gone up to the woods to find?"

"Happen. I'd like it better if there was another way, though."

Jasper drained his mug. "Such as? Look, Brew, the wench is alive and up at the castle, but I reckons now as she can't have seen us, else we'd have been took long since. But York's up there, and he's alive. *He's* the one as we've got to fear, for we *knows* as he saw us. I 'ad a friend once, 'it his damn fool head and was laid out for a week. Then he got up, grand as you like, like nothing'd 'appened. That there York might do just the same." He smiled. "But that fancy carriage 'ave got to get all the way to Hereford, all of a day's journey. Th'army won't be 'ere afore sometime tomorrow. My lads, we got all tonight to attend to York."

Jacob swallowed. "But, Jasper, we know as the leech saw us at the grave last night! What if he got that there housekeeper of 'is to look an' all? He en't daft, 'e knows as 'is word won't be took by itself no more."

Jasper grinned at Brew. "That Prissy Davies? Well, Brew, my handsome, that's *your* corner of the woods, en' it?"

"Aw, but, Jasper—"

"She've been sweet on you long enough, Brew. You make sure as she gets a little cuddling—she'll not admit to anything then, will she? Eh?"

Jacob sniggered, falling silent as Brew's cold eyes swung to him. Jasper brought more ale. "Tonight then. We'll 'ave to get on up to that there castle."

"An' just walk in, I suppose?" said Jacob. "Over the drawbridges as large as life!"

"No, my fool of a brother. There's another way in, one as everyone's 'eard of but never seen in many a year."

Jacob's eyes widened with fear. "No, Jasper, not through there, I couldn't! No one'd dare go there!"

"You'd rather swing, would you? I'll tek on ghosties any day afore I'd tek a rope neckerchief. Brew've found it, Jacob, and we'm goin' to get rid of those as is dangerous to us once and for all. Work it out, the black feller and the wench can't know anything. 'Tis just York. Without 'im they got nothin' on us. Without 'im—" He paused, grinning. "Without 'im, we got all them sparklin' diamonds to usselves, and our passage to America. We'm goin' to be rich, my laddos—but not if we messes up tonight, for tonight be our only chance!"

Chapter 25

It was the middle of the afternoon when, quite suddenly, the wind abated. Perhaps it happened gradually, but to Mally it seemed that it was abrupt, as if someone had closed a door. She took a thick shawl and went up the damp, worn steps leading up to the walk around the curtain wall. From there she could look over the entire valley, and beyond.

Llanglyn crouched by the ford, and wisps of smoke rose steadily in the windless air. In the park close to the castle they were burning parts of the chestnut tree and the wood smoke smelled sweet as it drifted over her. The sky was still gray, but it was lighter as if just through a thin layer of moisture the sun might be shining. She had stood here with Daniel once, on the day they pretended to be the lord and lady of Castell Melyn—

Now you are my damsel, Mally. But first you've got to pay a forfeit—

Oh, Daniel, I don't want to.

A forfeit, Mally.

She could see him now, his light brown hair and laughing eyes, holding the wooden sword he had made from two pieces of willow lashed together with reeds.

A forfeit, Mally. A proper forfeit.

She shivered, pushing her hair back as one stray breath of breeze wandered around the battlements. The flag stirred slightly and then fell back. The spire of St. Crispin's rose from the cluster of roofs in the valley and she could see the dark green patches of the yew trees in the churchyard. Daniel was down there now, not up here at the castle—

Maria came along the walk and leaned next to her. "Deep in thought, sister mine?"

"I was remembering, that's all."

"Daniel?"

"Yes."

"It's two years, Mally—"

"I know."

"That's what it was with you and Chris, wasn't it?"

Mally smiled. "Well, he won't have the same problem with Annabel."

"No, she'll not give him a run for his money, will she?" Maria looked at her.

"Chris doesn't like being given runs for his money—not unless his money rests on a Newmarket nag or a bruiser in a boxing booth. They'll do very well together, will Chris and Annabel."

Maria pulled a face. "It sounds boring."

"If it suits them then that's the way it should be, surely. We cannot *all* be swept from our feet by dashing young Americans with soulful eyes and winning ways. How is he?"

"Andrew? The same. Oh, Mally, he must recover, he *must!*"

Mally put her arm around her. "He will, I'm sure of it."

"Well, at least he will soon be able to come down from

that tower room and lie in a more comfortable bed. We had to put him up there, you know, when that dreadful vicar, the Reverend Iorwerth Jones, came calling unexpectedly one day. Richard thought it best to put Andrew somewhere where no one could happen upon him unexpectedly. Still, once the Turneys and Brew Darril are taken by the army, it will all be over. Most of it, anyway. Oh, they *must* be found guilty, Mally!"

"I'm sure they will be, sweeting."

"They should hang for what they did to Mrs. Harmon. And to Andrew." Maria blinked as the tears filled her eyes, and she stared down at the town. "If they aren't arrested—"

"You'll what?" asked Mally, smiling fondly.

"I'll burn down the Three Feathers!"

"I believe you would, too. Anyway, you won't have to resort to such measures, for Chris will convince the army commander at Abergavenny that he must come and that will be the end of it."

Maria shivered, for the autumn air was cold. "I should never have run away, you know. I could kick myself now. But, as usual, I just didn't think beyond the immediate problem. I didn't consider Mother, you, *or* of making Jasper suspicious. It would have worked but for my idiocy. Jasper would have been content that he was safe—and we could have tried to—to—" She broke off, biting her lip.

"And in the meantime Jasper might have felt so secure that he robbed and murdered someone else. It's better this way, Maria."

"Perhaps. Anyway, at least by this time tomorrow I shall have been able to make my peace with Mother. Or tried to, for I think she'll disown me when she knows I'm carrying Andrew's child."

"I won't disown you. You'll always have a home with me, you know that."

Maria smiled. "You're the best sister in the world. And I'm surely the worst. A fine pair."

"And both of us the bane of Llanglyn Court, that's a fact. There's Richard coming back." Mally watched the figure on the dun horse riding up the drive.

"Where's he been?"

"To argue with the farrier about the quality of his work!"

"That'll please Harry Finsby." Maria laughed.

"It's about time someone told that old crook a few home truths, and I rather think Richard was in the mood for a good argument today."

The hooves clattered beneath the barbican and into the courtyard, echoing around the castle. Maria turned to look at him as he dismounted.

"He's very handsome, don't you think, Mally?"

"Yes."

"He's very impressed with you, you know." Maria glanced at her. "Most taken, I would say."

Mally flushed. "He has a silver tongue."

"He wasn't trying to impress *me,* or charm *me.* I'm just his friend. I like to think I'm his good friend, and I know that I owe him a great deal for all he's tried to do for me. That's why—"

"Yes?"

"That's why I'm telling you."

"Are you matchmaking?" Mally was still looking at Richard. He was talking to the head groom and had taken off his top hat. It slapped against his thigh with each word, and then he bent to lift the horse's off foreleg, pointing out something.

"Matchmaking?" murmured Maria. "Yes, never more fervently in my life." She smiled then. "It'll be dark soon."

"Let's go in then."

"I—I think I'll go back to Andrew." Maria watched

Richard cross the courtyard and go in through the buttery door. "I would say, Mally, that there will be a splendid warm fire in the solar, don't you think?"

She hurried back along the wall walk and down the steps into the shadows of the courtyard. Richard's horse was being led away. Some rooks wheeled overhead, calling to one another, and another small breath of wind moved the flag again.

As Mally left the walk, she heard the sound of the drawbridge being raised and she paused in surprise. Why bother with that?

Chapter 26

Richard sat on the sofa by the fire, his long legs stretched out before him and a glass of cognac in his hand. He swirled it slowly, staring thoughtfully at the rich amber liquid. As Mally came in he made to stand, but she stopped him.

"You look so deep in thought I hate to disturb you. Is there some of that Madeira left? Oh, yes—" She crossed to the small table, conscious that she was blushing and that she was talking unnecessarily.

She took a seat opposite him. "Why have you had the drawbridge raised?"

"A precaution."

"Against what?"

"I'm not sure." He smiled. "Is that double Dutch?"

"A little."

"Well, Nathaniel told me something when I was in Llanglyn. His housekeeper came to him after luncheon, she was nervous and embarrassed. She said that if asked by anyone about the grave last night, she would deny that she had seen anything."

Mally's eyes widened. "But why?"

"We don't know for sure. Nathaniel saw Brew Darril with her earlier, though."

"Ah. Prissy Davies has carried a candle for Brew for as long as I can remember. He's steered well clear of her, though."

"Until now."

"Yes." Mally took a long breath. "A strange coincidence."

"Too strange." Richard stood, leaning one hand against the chimney breast and staring at one of the firedogs. "And put together with something else— When I was in Harry Finsby's forge, I heard two women talking outside. One said something about *them going up there tonight*. They began to walk away from the forge and I couldn't hear any more, so I went to see who they were. One was Turney's wife. The other looked so much like Brew Darril that she *has* to be his sister."

She nodded. "Ginny Darril."

He pushed a log more firmly on the fire with his boot. "Well, altogether I feel happier with the drawbridge *up* tonight. I'd dearly like to be sure where *up there* meant, though."

"You believe it's here, don't you?"

"Yes. I think somehow or other Jasper's got wind of why Chris and Annabel have left here today. Nathaniel coming up here first thing in the morning, perhaps— Or maybe he had someone follow the landau to see which road it took, and when it made for Abergavenny, he'd need no more prompting, would he?"

"Well, Jasper can't just walk into the castle, can he? Nor can he take it by storm."

He smiled at her. "That's what worries me. If he's coming up here, it's to find Andrew. But he knows he'll first have to get across the park, assuming he climbs the wall. Then he has to get into the castle itself. Even he cannot be that desperate that he intends an out-and-out—" He didn't finish, but went to pour some more cognac. "Mally, something's bothering me, and I can't put a finger on it."

"But what? If the drawbridge is up, then he cannot get in. Our forebears knew what they were about when it came to building impregnable fortresses, especially fortresses on the Welsh border. There isn't any other way into Castell Melyn."

"How do we know that?"

She stared and then shrugged. "Well, surely, if there was, you'd have discovered it by now."

"I haven't discovered everything about this place yet. To begin with, I don't know where it was that Daniel left you. Somewhere low, damp, and *long*? There just isn't anywhere like that here." Slowly he put the stopper back in the decanter. "That's what's bothering me," he said softly. "Your blasted hidey-hole sounds suspiciously like a tunnel."

She got slowly to her feet. A tunnel.

"Think back, Mally. Was it a tunnel?"

"I don't know, I can't remember."

"Try."

She went to the windows and drew a curtain back with one hand. It was quite dark outside now and she could see her own face looking back from the latticed glass, a face fragmented by the different small panes. What had happened that day when she and Daniel had come up here to the castle?

Richard put his glass down and came over to stand by her. "You described it before, Mally. Low, damp, and long. Was there anything else?"

"It was so dark. I couldn't see anything." She closed her eyes. "I just kept edging further and further up."

"Up? Steps?"

"No. A slope. A long, long slope upwards."

"More and more like a tunnel." He smiled ruefully,

putting a hand to the nape of her neck. "Try to think how you and Daniel got into it." His fingers moved gently in her hair.

A forfeit, Mally. A proper forfeit.

But why are we leaving the castle? Where are you taking me?

She turned to look at Richard. "Outside the castle, we went out past the lodge, I remember."

"I was afraid you might say that. So, Jasper knows your tunnel too."

"But I don't know where it is. Daniel blindfolded me—"

You mustn't see, Mally, that's part of the forfeit.

Promise you won't leave me.

Promise me, promise me, riddle me riddle me ree—

She shivered and dropped the curtain, shutting off the echoing voices.

Richard sighed. "Daniel was too damned efficient, wasn't he? He must have been a loathsome brat."

She laughed slightly. "He was. I worshiped him, though."

"Yes, well I suppose he went through some metamorphosis, for he was tolerable when I knew him." He smiled at her, taking her hand and drawing her toward the fire. "Sit down again, and we'll think about where the tunnel *ends* then."

"I don't know." She said it quickly and she didn't know why.

He sat next to her on the sofa, looked curiously at her. "Don't snap my head off."

"I didn't mean to." She reached out to him. "I don't know why I said it like that."

His fingers wrapped around hers. "You don't want to think about it, that's why."

"But I do—"

"No, your memory doesn't. It's something Nathaniel

said. And Stiller, for that matter. They are of the theory, the controversial theory, that, sometimes, the mind shuts away things it doesn't want to think about. Upsetting things. For you it is that day in the tunnel. For Andrew it is the night Mrs. Harmon was murdered."

She was disbelieving. "If that's the case we should be able to conveniently forget anything we choose."

"That's what I said. But, they believe it to be so. Stiller propounds most eloquently on the subject."

She smiled. "Someone should tell the Prince of Wales, then perhaps Princess Caroline would vanish from the face of the earth for him."

"He's doing all he can to that end already, without Dr. Stiller's fearsome theories. Anyway, the tunnel. What *do* you remember? Your father rescued you, didn't he? Isn't that what you said?"

"Yes. He wrapped a blanket around me in the courtyard. He came alone, he didn't want the whole neighborhood to know about what had happened."

"But he knew where to come?"

"Daniel told him. He confessed he'd left me there. He was thrashed so much he could hardly walk, I remember that."

"Mally. You're in the courtyard with your father. How did you get there?"

She looked at him. "I can't remember." She bit her lip and lowered her eyes, shaking her head. "I just can't remember. I'm sorry, Richard—"

He pulled her closer, his arm around her. "Don't look so woebegone, it plays havoc with me. Well, at least we know there *is* a tunnel, that it begins *outside* the castle, and ends *inside* it. And you can bet your grandmother's mobcap that friend Jasper knows it too."

"But why hasn't he used it before then?"

"I don't know." He looked at the fire. "There'll be a reason, but I can't think what. Perhaps he didn't finally make up his mind until he looked in the grave. It doesn't matter what his reasons are, I'm pretty sure he's intending using it tonight. There's nothing for it but to search every cellar."

She smiled. "Perhaps Gwynneth could ask Lady Jacquetta."

"Gwynneth?"

"Oh yes, she sees our ghostly lady quite often, so she tells me."

"A maid with second sight? I suppose that's all this night lacks. That and a few unearthly howls and the dry rattle of bones."

Her smile faded. "Don't say that."

He put his hand to her cheek. "I hadn't imagined I was creating quite such an effect, forgive me—"

"It was the bones," she whispered.

"What bones?"

"In the tunnel." She put her hand over his, gripping his fingers tightly as she remembered. "When father's lantern shone on me from above, I saw them. Bones. Human bones."

The screams came winging back over the years, echoing around and around in her head, childish screams of terror. And the swinging, dancing light of the lantern as her father climbed down— She put her hands over her ears, but the memories seemed only to grow louder.

Richard caught her close, holding her gently.

"I kept screaming. I screamed and screamed. And I couldn't move, I was so terrified. Oh, God, I was terrified. I must have fainted, for that's all I remember." She sat back weakly, her mouth dry. "It's so vivid it has the power to frighten me even now. But there's one thing we know now. If I did faint when Father found me, then that's why I don't know how he got me out or where it was."

"We might find it tonight, I'll have every man search.

The women can stay in the kitchens together. You go up into the tower with Maria, and lock yourself in that top room. All right?"

"Yes." She stood.

He went to the corner table where Annabel had left her book the night before. "Here, take this. Annabel said that it had a lot more detail of Lady Jacquetta's story—perhaps there is something in there about a tunnel. Faint hope, but hope nonetheless."

She nodded, taking the book. As she reached the door, he spoke again. "I love you, Mally."

She looked back at him, and her hand dropped from the door handle. She went back to him. "And I love you, Richard," she whispered.

He pulled her into his arms and kissed her. As she held him she knew that this time it was different. With Chris it had been a shadow. With Daniel something she would always cherish. But with Richard—

He smiled. "You're all mine, Mally. *I'll* not share you."

"You won't have to."

Chapter 27

Maria's hands twisted together on the edge of Andrew's bed. "Maybe Richard's wrong, maybe Jasper *isn't* coming."

"Maybe." Mally put the marker in the page and closed the book for a moment, rubbing her eyes.

"You don't sound reassuring."

"I can't help it, I think he's right. I only hope he can find the end of the tunnel first—"

"I never could stand Daniel St. Aubrey as a child. It must have been a premonition of this!"

"Daniel *was* pretty awful at times, wasn't he?" Mally opened the book again, smiling. "I can't think why Annabel was so engrossed in this book, there doesn't seem anything interesting in it."

"What did she say?"

"Well, she said she wouldn't go into the same *gruesome* detail the book did about Lady Jacquetta's fate."

"Then there must be something there. Read on, Marigold."

"Mother wouldn't thank you for that mimicry."

Maria smiled faintly and took Andrew's hand, putting

it against her cheek. "Please, Andrew, *please!*" she murmured, resting her other hand against his long fair hair.

For a long time the room was silent. The candle guttered, and Mally looked up at it. "I can't read any more of this lettering, Maria. You'll have to do it for a while."

"Me?"

"Yes. You were always better at such things than I was anyway."

"Because I liked our tutor."

"The handsome young Mr. Blatchford? You terrified him. Anyway, the book is yours. Here."

Maria took it and went to the other bed, lying down and resting her chin on one hand. "From the page you've marked?"

"Yes."

"And nothing's happened so far?"

"John of Gaunt has sojourned with his vast retinue and eaten poor Lord Whoever-it-was-at-the-time out of house and home. But apparently it was worth it for the Duke's favor."

Mally went to the tiny window and looked out. The stars winked in a clear sky and the moon's silver light lay over the valley. The castle was quiet. Shouldn't there be more noise? She opened the window and immediately felt foolish. She would hardly hear the sounds of searching going on in the cellars—

"At last. Lady Jacquetta."

She turned to look at Maria. "What does it say?"

"Just a minute, I'll read all of it and then tell you." Maria turned another two pages and then closed the book. "I think I know why Annabel wouldn't read it to you—"

"Well? Oh, come on, don't lie there knowing it all without telling me!"

"Lady Jacquetta was being unfaithful to her husband, Sir Francis, with a certain nobleman from Court named

Sir Piers. Piers and Francis were both adherents of Richard III. Oh, it's 1485. The year of Bosworth and all that."

"Yes." Mally controlled her impatience.

"When Francis discovered what had been going on, he had Jacquetta thrown in the dungeon. He was so furious about it that he demanded justice from the king, but poor Richard had problems enough—he didn't dare mete out anything to Piers because he needed as much support as he could for the invading Henry Tudor was making noises across the Channel. Francis was beside himself with a sense of the injustice of it all. He changed his allegiance to Henry. Castell Melyn was important, because it was one route into England which Henry might take, so Richard rather tactlessly dispatched none other than Piers to lay siege to the castle."

"Is there any mention of a tunnel at all, or does it ramble on like this?"

"There's a tunnel. But I have to tell you everything in the right order. Now, where had I got to?"

"Piers is about to lay siege to Castell Melyn."

"Oh, yes. Well he *did* lay siege to it. And Francis sat tight, leaving Jacquetta in the dungeon still, for he was more determined than ever now to punish her. That was a little poetic license on my part—I haven't a clue what his intentions about her were. The siege hadn't been in progress very long when one day Piers's men found a spring on the mountain below the castle, and when they knelt to use it, they saw that behind the rock it came from beneath, there was a space. When they pulled the rock away they found the entrance to a cave."

Why does it echo in here, Daniel?

The words were in Mally's head immediately and she could hear her own stumbling footsteps again. And the vague gurgle of water.

Maria sat up. "The cave went a long way back into the

hill, and Piers had the capital notion of helping the cave on its way by digging a tunnel and perhaps managing to get into the castle. And this is what he did. Each day, when there were exchanges of cannonfire or whatever between the castle and the besieging force, some of Piers's men were making their way nearer and nearer to the castle. Then word came from the king that Piers and his force were needed, but Piers was anxious to get to Jacquetta if he could, so he told his men to tunnel at night as well, and that was his mistake. The guards watching over Jacquetta heard the sounds. Francis knew immediately what was going on. He decided on what Annabel must mean by the *gruesome* part of it. The next day he had his men begin firing cannonade after cannonade at Piers's men, guessing that Piers would be forced to withdraw a little, taking all his men with him. Then he took up the floor of the dungeon and had his own men dig down to meet the tunnel. His stonemasons built a solid wall across the tunnel, underneath the dungeon. He then—he then chained Jacquetta behind the new wall and replaced the floor of the dungeon. When all was done, he relaxed the castle's onslaught. And waited. Piers advanced to his former position again and sent his men to continue. He had had another command from the king, and was desperate for Jacquetta. His men went up to the tunnel and found a wall where there shouldn't be one. And they heard Jacquetta's pitiful moans the other side. They were so terrified they went back out again. Piers couldn't get one of his men to go into the tunnel, and so decided he would obey the king's orders and lift the siege. Jacquetta was left there forever."

"The dungeon. That's where it is—" Mally ran to the door and began to unbolt it.

"Don't go, Mally!" Maria was suddenly frightened. "That's the first place Richard will look—"

"I must tell him, it's important." The door crashed

back as Mally forced the bolts at last, gathering her skirts to run down the winding steps.

The draught set the candle flickering wildly. Maria turned to shield it, but it was too late. The room was in darkness suddenly and the air filled with the smell of the candle. The door at the foot of the tower crashed as Mally ran out. Trembling, Maria remained where she was, afraid to cross to the door. The steps led down into darkness, and the cold sweep of air from the courtyard below passed over her as if it sensed her fear.

A light appeared down the steps. A tiny light, a candle protected by someone's hand, someone who crept up the steps very slowly. Maria's eyes widened, and she was frozen, unable to make her legs or arms move. She stared at the light, so pink as it glowed through the fingers. As the top of the steps was reached Maria screamed.

"Miss Maria? Miss Maria, it's only me. Gwynneth. I saw your light had gone out—"

Maria pressed the back of her hand against her mouth, shaking so much she couldn't speak. Gwynneth came closer, holding the new candle to the old one, and then she crouched beside Maria. "I didn't mean to frighten you, Miss Maria. Look now, take some of this wine you've left in the glass, it will help you. Oh, but your hands are so cold." Gwynneth held the glass out and Maria took it. As she did so she looked across at Andrew.

He smiled at her.

Louis was holding a lantern in the dungeon, and Richard was crouching on the floor looking down into a hole. Light from another lantern glowed up from the hole, lighting Richard's face.

"What do you see, Abel?" He turned as Mally came down the steps. "We've just found it."

"It was in Annabel's book." She remained by the door, unwilling to go nearer.

"Come and lay your nightmare, Mally." He held out his hand. "Come on."

She slowly crossed and took his hand. The lantern light wavered over the second dungeon, just as it had when her father had found her. A wave of revulsion swept over her and she drew away, but Richard held her firmly.

"This was where he buried her," she whispered, "where he left her to die." She stared past Abel at the wall which Francis had built. The chain still hung rustily from the stonework, but the stonework itself had crumbled in one place, revealing the yawning, empty blackness of the tunnel. Her eyes went to the chain again, following it down to the foot of the wall. All that remained of Jacquetta still lay there, white and pitiful. Mally stood, swallowing.

But at that moment Abel extinguished his lantern. "Someone coming, Mas' Vallender!" He turned and thrust the lantern back up into Richard's hand, and Richard reached down to pull him up. Quickly they dragged the flagstone back into place.

"Damn! If we only knew the other end of the tunnel, we could keep them in there until Chris gets back!" Richard took Mally's hand again. "Did it say in the book?"

"It starts in a cave. A cave behind a spring."

Abel nodded. "Maybe *I* know, Mas' Vallender."

"Take some men with you then, and some pistols. A shot or two should keep our friends well and truly in the cave. Hurry then."

"I send someone back if we got them, Mas' Vallender." Abel hurried from the dungeon, and Richard took Mally's arm.

"We'll bolt the dungeon door. Come on."

Louis followed them with the lantern and Richard dragged the old door to, bolting it firmly.

"That'll hold them. That and the door up into the courtyard."

MALLY

Outside in the clear moonlit night, Mally shivered, partly from the cold and partly from the excitement.

Gwynneth hurried across toward them. "Mr. Vallender, Mr. Vallender, it's Mr. York. He's woken up!"

Richard hugged Mally. "Now, all we need is for Abel to send back that he's got them trapped in the tunnel!"

"Is he all right, Gwynneth?" asked Mally.

The maid nodded. "He's weak, ma'am, and I'm fetching some good broth now. But he knows Miss Maria, he said her name. Oh, and he asked if they'd caught Jasper Turney yet, caught him for murdering Mrs. Harmon."

Maria still didn't know whether to laugh or cry when Richard and Mally came up. She sat by Andrew, holding his hand tightly.

Richard grinned at Andrew. "You took your time, you sonofa———!"

Andrew smiled. "If I weren't so goddamn weak—"

"You and whose army?" Richard stood at the foot of the bed. "Do you remember, Andrew?"

"Yes. I saw them through the window. I heard her scream. The moon came out and I saw them do it. But they saw me at the same time. Have you got them?"

A horse clattered into the courtyard below and Mally went to the top of the steps. One of the grooms came up, looking up to where she stood, her figure lit by the candles in the room behind her.

"We've caught them, Mrs. St. Aubrey. Abel had the right place."

She turned. "We've got them, Mr. York."

Chapter 28

Several days later the Turneys and Brew Darril were in custody at Hereford, and the township of Llanglyn was ringing with the tale of what had really happened on the night Agatha Harmon had died, and there were a considerable number of shamed faces to be seen around the streets and marketplace.

But up at Castell Melyn, late on a sunny autumn afternoon, it was quiet.

Mally stood alone by Gillian Vallender's portrait. Richard's dead wife stared out from the canvas, remote and lovely.

"Gillie was a fine-looking woman," said a voice behind her, and she turned to see Andrew York standing there.

"You startled me," she said, for somehow it was almost like looking at Gillian to see his pale fair face. And those bright blue eyes—

"I'm sorry, I didn't mean to creep up on you, but this old place sure has that effect on me. I feel I *must* be stealthy." He grinned.

"How are you feeling now?"

"Well. I'm more concerned now about Maria."

"She's as healthy as ever, you don't need to worry about her."

He nodded up at the portrait. "Gillie died in childbed. I have to worry about Maria."

"Looking at this portrait, I would guess that Gillian was not as hale and healthy as my sister."

"Looking at that portrait you would not guess *anything* about my late cousin." He came closer, studying the canvas. "It was painted only a year before she died, you know. Before then, the artist would have captured a different woman entirely."

"What do you mean?"

He looked at her, his blue eyes shrewd. "I will tell you the truth about her, Mally—I may call you that?"

"If you are to marry my sister I should hope you would."

"Right, Mally. I will tell you, because I have already noticed you here several times, looking at Gillie. But what I say is between you, me, and the last bayou."

"The last what?"

"It doesn't matter. You, me, and the doorpost then. Richard thinks he married Gillie because he was sorry for her, because she was shackled to old man York's plantation more than any slave, and because he wanted to rescue her. Maybe it's true, in a way. But Gillie was no delicate blossom, not by a long way. Her life *was* stifling, but not that much. Her father intended marrying her to the son of a neighboring owner, a family of French extraction. More than anything else in the world Gillie wanted *out* of that betrothal. Richard happened along at the perfect time, and she knew how to play a part. We Yorks are adept at that part, Mally, for I used the same ploy myself on your sister." He smiled at her startled face. "I wanted Maria more than anything else in the world, and I knew how to catch her eye, her interest, and her heart. The Yorks look soulful, like spaniel puppies, but we're far from that."

"So it would seem."

"The difference between my action and Gillie's is that I was in love with Maria. Gillie didn't love Richard. At least, not at first. In the end she did. He married her because he liked her, because he was sorry for her, and because in the end it would bring him Le Bosquet Bas—*I'm* the son of a third or fourth brother, and don't count, I'm afraid. Old man York was so mad he had a fit when she and Richard got married. Right under his nose, it was, in the fanciest church in New Orleans. But, it was done, and he was powerless to do anything but grit his teeth and smile. Or make everything over to me, which he would never do in a month of wet Sundays, as he regarded my mother as a whore, if you'll excuse the word. She was an actress, and no one born of *her* was to get his hands on Le Bosquet Bas. So, Richard was welcomed home. Within a year old man York was dead anyway. Fever. And by then my cousin had realized that she was desperately in love with her British husband. She had hidden her true self from him, Mally, because she knew that he would not have liked her true self. Mally—Gillie had throughout her life been hard, grasping, spiteful, and selfish. And that is no exaggeration."

Mally stared at him. "Surely not." She then looked up at the sweet face in the portrait.

"That face you see there is Gillie not long before she died, when she was in love with Richard. She knew she would never have him, not completely. Damn it, I liked her then, I'd hated her before. She'd become unhappy. And she'd softened."

"Richard didn't make her unhappy."

"No, he didn't, he was the perfect husband, if such a beast exists. He didn't love her, though. I sat on the wall between them, watching both and knowing more about each than the other did."

"Richard thinks she never knew he didn't love her."

"I know. She did, though. The knowledge that she was having his child brought her great joy. What might have happened if she had lived—and the little girl—I don't know. But you don't have to look over your shoulder at Gillie Vallender, Mally. Richard's yours, absolutely and completely. Just as you are his. There's no Daniel St. Aubrey now, is there?"

"No."

"Then why worry about poor Gillie? She can't touch him now any more than she could then. Let's have only one ghost at Castell Melyn—the late, departed Lady Jacquetta de Winter."

She smiled at him. "I can understand how you absolutely devastated my sister, Andrew York—to use my mother's words."

"It's my American charm and boyish beauty."

"Obviously."

He kissed her cheek. "Go on, go to Richard and forget Gillie."

"And give in to my baser feelings as you and Maria did?" she murmured, smiling at him.

"Ah—now that's entirely up to you. Between you, me, and—"

"The last bayou."

Annabel knelt beside the little mound of fresh earth and put a bunch of pink chrysanthemums beside the little wooden cross. "There, Lady Jacquetta," she said, "may you rest in peace after all this time."

Gwynneth bent quickly and put some Christmas roses next to the other bouquet. *"Ffarwel,"* she whispered.

"A fitting end to all this, don't you think?" asked Chris.

Mally smiled at him. "Yes, and an ending I did not expect for one moment. Andrew is better and Maria happy beyond all reason, and you and Annabel are together. It is all as it should be."

He slipped an arm around her shoulder. "And you and Richard?"

"I love him, Chris."

He looked at her. "I can see that you do—you never looked at me the way you look at him. Damn his eyes. But I wish you both well—you know that, don't you?"

She nodded.

"So," he said, "when Richard returns from Hereford today, we shall celebrate."

At that moment Annabel leaped to her feet, looking around with wide eyes. "Something touched my shoulder!"

"There's nothing there," said Chris.

Gwynneth smiled. "She was only saying good-bye and thank you."

"Who?" asked Annabel.

"Why Lady Jacquetta, of course. She won't be back again now, for she can rest happily after all this time." The little maid bobbed a curtsey and hurried back toward the castle.

Annabel stood there, looking from Chris to Mally.

Chris laughed. "Well, don't stand there looking like that. After all, that *is* why you came here."

"I didn't really believe in it," she said at last. "Not *really*." She looked down at the grave for a long moment.

Mally smiled at Chris. "Take heart, my friend, for I fancy that's the last ghost-hunt you'll ever be dragged on!"

Mrs. Berrisford sat gingerly in the solar, looking around carefully. "Most exquisite," she said at last, sniffing once.

Richard smiled at her. "I take that as a compliment, Mrs. Berrisford."

"Indeed, Mr. Vallender. Oh, dear, this is all most embarrassing, for I do not know how to address you. I have been mistaken in the past, most mistaken, and for that I apologize. However—"

"Mother!" Mally stood beside Richard. "There is no *however* about it. For goodness' sake, be gracious."

"I'm trying, Marigold, believe me. But after receiving Maria's most distressing news—"

"Distressing? But everything is going to be all right, they will be married next week—"

"Yes, and the child born rather too soon after that date for my comfort. What *will* everyone say? And there's that dreadful Mrs. Clevely calling upon me tomorrow. Word's reached her, you know. Some idle toad of a gossip went whispering to the old dragon."

"Refuse to see her." Mally looked at her mother patiently. "Or see her and spit in her eye."

"Marigold!"

"Well, as if it matters what that old biddy has to say! She's a nothing!" She smiled then. "Anyway, if Maria and Andrew marry up in London, how is anyone down here going to know *when* they were married? Mm?"

Mrs. Berrisford smiled slowly. "My *dear,* I hadn't thought of that! Of course, they could have married months ago. Absolutely *months!*" The smile faded. "But then there's the matter of your engagement to Sir Christopher."

Richard took Mally's hand. "I'm afraid, Mrs. Berrisford, that the name of Vallender carries little of the shine carried by that of Carlyon."

"But it's not *that* which concerns me, Mr. Vallender," said Mrs. Berrisford, looking hurt. "It's that people might say *he* threw Marigold over in favor of Lady Annabel!"

"Oh, mother, for heaven's sake—"

"Don't blaspheme, Marigold."

"You drive me to it. If *I* don't care what people say, I really don't know why you do. If you like, I'll rush Richard to the altar as quickly as Maria is rushing—now *that* would give the gossips something to chew over."

"That will not be necessary, Marigold. As you say, if you don't care, why should I? That's the end of it then. I congratulate you both."

Mally took a long breath. "Don't fall over yourself with enthusiasm, Mother."

"It just takes a little getting used to, that's all. Well, really, if you *must* know I've been embroidering some bed linen with the initials *M* and *C*. Now I'll have to unpick it all! It's too much, really it is."

Mally smiled, going to the plump, red-wigged figure and putting her arms around her. "Give them to Chris and Annabel for a wedding gift. *M* and *C*. Murchison and Carlyon. It's perfect."

"Marigold, how absolutely splendid. Now I shall not have to sit up night after night unpicking. I do so hate unpicking." Mrs. Berrisford beamed. "And I didn't like the colors I'd chosen anyway. Yellow and green. Not the thing. No, now it shall be oyster and white on cream sheets. Yes, and the initials *M* and *R*."

"Mother, do you remember the day Daniel left me in that tunnel?"

"Why, yes, my dear. Your father and Daniel's father spent a good deal of time up here putting the floor of the dungeon back into place. And they pushed a boulder across the entrance of the tunnel down in the woods. And to think that dreadful Brew Darril sniffed it out after all that time. Oh, *what* might have happened if those three ruffians had got in here, I dread to think—still, poor dear Agatha's jewels have been recovered and have gone to their rightful owner. Agatha had a niece, you know. Mind you—" There was another sniff. "The gel never came near her old aunt. Not once. Agatha couldn't stand the wench."

"Now who's being a gossip?"

Mrs. Berrisford smiled sleekly. "It's one of the greatest pleasures in life, child. You'll find that out in the end, even from up here in this drafty castle. Gossip and chitter-chatter. The most feared and most enjoyed pastime. Well, perhaps *almost* the most enjoyed." She pulled Mally a little closer and whispered in her ear. "Do you know, Marigold, he's even more good-looking than Sir Christopher, but when I look at him I just can't think how. Charming. One can imagine some most enjoyable pastimes with him, don't you know."

"Mother! I'm surprised at you."

"Why? Even I have my memories. Now then, take yourselves for that walk. I'm going to the kitchens to see how that Creole cook produces those dishes. Pattie will have to master that particular art, if it kills me."

Lucy walked among the trees, and the deer took little notice of her slow figure.

Mally and Richard watched her and Mally slipped her hand into his. "There, she *will* be here when the daffodils are out again after all."

"She seemed quite overcome when the landau came over the lodge drawbridge."

"She was." Mally looked up at him and smiled. "Mother was right, you know—one *can* imagine wickedly pleasing ways of passing the time with you."

His dark eyes glittered. "I can help you do more than *imagine* them, sweetheart!"

"Ah, but think of losing all that delicious anticipation."

"The hell with anticipation."

ABOUT THE AUTHOR

SANDRA HEATH was born in 1944. As the daughter of an officer in the Royal Air Force, most of her life was spent traveling around to various European posts. She has lived and worked in both Holland and Germany.

The author now resides in Gloucester, England, together with her husband and young daughter, where all her spare time is spent writing. She is especially fond of exotic felines and, at one time or another, has owned each breed of cat.

SIGNET Books by Clare Darcy

- **ALLEGRA** (#E7851—$1.75)
- **CRESSIDA** (#E8287—$1.75)*
- **ELYZA** (#E7540—$1.75)
- **EUGENIA** (#E8081—$1.75)
- **GWENDOLEN** (#J8847—$1.95)*
- **LADY PAMELA** (#W7282—$1.50)
- **LYDIA** (#E8272—$1.75)
- **REGINA** (#E7878—$1.75)
- **ROLANDE** (#J8552—$1.95)
- **VICTOIRE** (#E7845—$1.75)

* Price slightly higher in Canada

Buy them at your local
bookstore or use coupon
on next page for ordering.

Big Bestsellers from SIGNET

- [ ] **THE PASSIONATE SAVAGE by Constance Gluyas.**
(#E9195—$2.50)*
- [ ] **MADAM TUDOR by Constance Gluyas.** (#J8953—$1.95)*
- [ ] **THE HOUSE ON TWYFORD STREET by Constance Gluyas.**
(#E8924—$2.25)*
- [ ] **FLAME OF THE SOUTH by Constance Gluyas.**
(#E8648—$2.50)
- [ ] **WOMAN OF FURY by Constance Gluyas.** (#E8075—$2.25)*
- [ ] **ROGUE'S MISTRESS by Constance Gluyas.** (#E8339—$2.25)
- [ ] **SAVAGE EDEN by Constance Gluyas.** (#E9285—$2.50)
- [ ] **OAKHURST by Walter Reed Johnson.** (#J7874—$1.95)
- [ ] **MISTRESS OF OAKHURST by Walter Reed Johnson.**
(#J8253—$1.95)
- [ ] **LION OF OAKHURST by Walter Reed Johnson.**
(#E8844—$2.25)*
- [ ] **FIRES OF OAKHURST by Walter Reed Johnson.**
(#E9406—$2.50)
- [ ] **REAP THE BITTER WINDS by June Lund Shiplett.**
(#E9517—$2.50)
- [ ] **THE RAGING WINDS OF HEAVEN by June Lund Shiplett.**
(#E9439—$2.50)
- [ ] **THE WILD STORMS OF HEAVEN by June Lund Shiplett.**
(#E9063—$2.50)*
- [ ] **DEFY THE SAVAGE WINDS by June Lund Shiplett.**
(#E9337—$2.50)*

*Price slightly higher in Canada

Buy them at your local bookstore or use this convenient coupon for ordering.

THE NEW AMERICAN LIBRARY, INC.
P.O. Box 999, Bergenfield, New Jersey 07621

Please send me the SIGNET BOOKS I have checked above. I am enclosing
$_____ (please add 50¢ to this order to cover postage and handling). Send check or money order—no cash or C.O.D.'s. Prices and numbers are subject to change without notice.

Name_____

Address_____

City_____ State_____ Zip Code_____
Allow 4-6 weeks for delivery.
This offer is subject to withdrawal without notice.

Recommended SIGNET Reading

- [ ] **THE ETRUSCAN SMILE by Velda Johnston.** (#E9020—$2.25)
- [ ] **CALENDAR OF SINNERS by Moira Lord.** (#J9021—$1.95)*
- [ ] **SUNSET by Christopher Nicole.** (#E8948—$2.25)*
- [ ] **A VERY CAGEY LADY by Joyce Elbert.** (#E9240—$2.75)*
- [ ] **THE CRAZY LOVERS by Joyce Elbert.** (#E8917—$2.75)*
- [ ] **THE CRAZY LADIES by Joyce Elbert.** (#E8923—$2.75)
- [ ] **MAKING IT by Bryn Chandler.** (#E8756—$2.25)*
- [ ] **JO STERN by David Slavitt.** (#J8753—$1.95)*
- [ ] **THE HOUSE OF KINGSLEY MERRICK by Deborah Hill.** (#E9818—$2.50)*
- [ ] **THIS IS THE HOUSE by Deborah Hill.** (#E8877—$2.50)
- [ ] **EYE OF THE NEEDLE by Ken Follett.** (#E8746—$2.95)
- [ ] **A GARDEN OF SAND by Earl Thompson.** (#E9374—$2.95)
- [ ] **TATTOO by Earl Thompson.** (#E8989—$2.95)
- [ ] **CALDO LARGO by Earl Thompson.** (#E7737—$2.25)
- [ ] **CITY OF WHISPERING STONE by George Chesbro.** (#J8812—$1.95)*
- [ ] **SHADOW OF A BROKEN MAN by George Chesbro.** (#J8114—$1.95)*

 * Price slightly higher in Canada

Buy them at your local
bookstore or use coupon
on next page for ordering.

More Bestsellers from SIGNET

- [ ] **SPHINX by Robin Cook.** (#E9194—$2.95)
- [ ] **COMA by Robin Cook.** (#E8202—$2.50)
- [ ] **LOVE IS NOT ENOUGH by Ruth Lyons.** (#E9196—$2.50)*
- [ ] **LET THE LION EAT STRAW by Elleasse Southerland.** (#J9201—$1.95)*
- [ ] **STARBRIAR by Lee Wells.** (#E9202—$2.25)*
- [ ] **BLOOD RITES by Barry Nazarian.** (#J9203—$1.95)*
- [ ] **SALT MINE by David Lippincott.** (#E9158—$2.25)*
- [ ] **SAVAGE RANSOM by David Lippincott.** (#E8749—$2.25)*
- [ ] **ROOMMATE by Jacqueline Wein.** (#E9160—$2.25)*
- [ ] **WINE OF THE DREAMERS by Susannah Leigh.** (#E9157—$2.95)
- [ ] **GLYNDA by Susannah Leigh.** (#E8548—$2.50)*
- [ ] **CLAUDINE'S DAUGHTER by Rosalind Laker.** (#E9159—$2.25)*
- [ ] **WARWYCK'S WOMAN by Rosalind Laker.** (#E8813—$2.25)*
- [ ] **THE MONEYMAN by Judith Liederman.** (#E9164—$2.75)*
- [ ] **SINS OF OMISSION by Chelsea Quinn Yarbro.** (#E9165—$2.25)*

*Price slightly higher in Canada

Buy them at your local bookstore or use this convenient coupon for ordering.

THE NEW AMERICAN LIBRARY, INC.,
P.O. Box 999, Bergenfield, New Jersey 07621

Please send me the SIGNET BOOKS I have checked above. I am enclosing
$_____ (please add 50¢ to this order to cover postage and handling).
Send check or money order—no cash or C.O.D.'s. Prices and numbers are
subject to change without notice.

Name _____

Address _____

City_____ State_____ Zip Code_____

Allow 4-6 weeks for delivery.
This offer is subject to withdrawal without notice.